PRAISE FOR THE UNRAVELLING OF OU

"Wildly original and captivating. A phenomenal examination of female shame, sexuality, queerness, motherhood, and intimacy, Hollay Ghadery writes with sensitivity and resonating beauty through an unconventional narrator: a sock puppet, Ecology Paul, who delivers the emotional coming-of-age tale of young Minoo with whimsy and emotional depth. Minoo feels trapped in her body and guilt over its sensual pleasures, as she grapples with a complicated relationship with a traditional Iranian mother. In *The Unravelling of Ou*, the immigrant Canadian narrative is dismantled, and headstrong mothers and daughters clash with patriarchal structures that want to control their bodies, their vanity, and their desires. Vulnerable, brave, and heartbreaking, this powerful novel asks: how do women function in a world that is not designed to love them back? How do oppressed individuals understand and ultimately save themselves? Ghadery delivers answers in a lyrical and imaginative debut."

— **LINDSAY WONG,** ***Villain Hitting for Vicious Little Nobodies***

"With poignant and delicate prose, *The Unravelling of Ou* draws the reader in through the unique voice of Minoo's puppet. Ou knows all the secrets for Ou lives inside Minoo, and only Ou can reveal the depth of the brutal choice forced upon Minoo by her mother when she was a little girl. It's a choice that shapes Minoo's life in irreversible ways, even after estrangement from its root cause. A daring, not-to-be-missed short novel by the one and only Hollay Ghadery."

— **NILOFAR-LILY SOLTANI,** ***Zulaikha***

"*The Unravelling of Ou* is wonderfully layered, with a compelling plot and deeply realized characters. Its bracingly effective central conceit—first person narration by the protagonist's sock puppet—is fresh and satisfying and, ultimately, quite moving."

K.R. WILSON, ***Call Me Stan*** **and** ***An Idea About My Dead Uncle***

"This novel is a delicious titration of acts of betrayal and care. I've never read anything like it before and yet it felt familiar in hard-to-reach places of the soul."

— MARGO LAPIERRE,
editor and author of *Ajar*

"Ghadery has written a surprising narrative that interrogates the treatment of young women caught in the crossfire of cultural norms and mental health. Beautifully told with her trademark use of evocative and poetic language, Ghadery has once again challenged readers to ponder identity and what it means to be seen."

— LUCY E.M. BLACK, *A Quilting of Scars, The Brickworks, Class Lessons: Stories of Vulnerable Youth*

"Hollay Ghadery explores the weighty and intricate realm of mother-daughter relationships in this exquisitely wrought story of one woman's struggle to love and accept herself despite her mother's betrayal, her self-recriminations, and later, her own daughter's disapproval. Ghadery cleverly employs the conceit of a sock puppet narrator, a tool the main character, Minoo, uses to replace the love and advice she craved from the mother who sent her away. Every detail, whether heartbreaking or healing, is handled with expert care. Ghadery's gamble, employing an inanimate and usually innocuous toy to explore the burdens of female biology — the pink innocence of widely-held perception versus the bloody, life-giving pain of reality — is a winning strategy. Ideas of femininity, desire, and sexuality are masterfully showcased without judgement, without recrimination. This book is a must-read."

— GINA LEOLA WOOLSEY, *Fifteen Thousand Pieces: A Medical Examiner's Journey Through Disaster*

THE UNRAVELLING OF OU

Palimpsest Press
1171 Eastlawn Ave.
Windsor, Ontario. N8S 3J1
www.palimpsestpress.ca

Printed and bound in Canada
Cover design and book typography by Ellie Hastings
Edited by Aimée Parent Dunn
Copyedited by Ashley Van Elswyk

Palimpsest Press would like to thank the Canada Council for the Arts and the Ontario Arts Council for their support of our publishing program. We also acknowledge the assistance of the Government of Ontario through the Ontario Book Publishing Tax Credit.

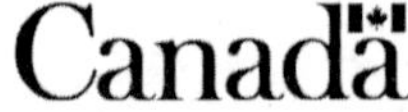

LIBRARY AND ARCHIVES CANADA CATALOGUING IN PUBLICATION

TITLE: The unravelling of ou / Hollay Ghadery.
NAMES: Ghadery, Hollay, author.
IDENTIFIERS: Canadiana (print) 20250306808
Canadiana (ebook) 20250310031

ISBN 9781997508090 (SOFTCOVER)
ISBN 9781997508106 (EPUB)
SUBJECTS: LCGFT: Novels.

CLASSIFICATION: LCC PS8613.H33 U57 2026 | DDC C813/.6—DC23

THE UNRAVELLING OF OU

HOLLAY GHADERY

To EP

"The increasing seriousness of things,
then that's the great opportunity of jokes."

—*Henry James*

IT'S NOT EVERY DAY A SOCK PUPPET VISITS A MATERNITY WARD

Minoo and I fly down the hall, the anticipated squeak of hospital vinyl absent from under our feet. We are weightless, shoes barely touching the ground. A reflection of Minoo's form glides beneath us. Wraith-like, we are darkly mirrored in the freshly-waxed floor.

And Minoo—she stares ahead, unseeing. Not seeing me, I mean. As conspicuous as I am to everyone else, my existence is as natural to her as the weight of her tongue in her mouth, or the air filling the lungs in her chest. She doesn't see the nurse who jumps out of our way either, flattening her body to the wall, blue eyes large with shock.

I know Minoo would rather cut off her arm than look at me. I can feel it. Her hand—her hand with the soft palm and short nails—is less of a hand now and more of a fist. Its metacarpal tension curls in my body. *Minoo.* I try to say her name, but she won't let me open my mouth.

Minoo. Listen to me.

Ahead, the elevator doors slide open, and a boy emerges with a bouquet of balloons. He looks at us as we pass, then turns to look again, a smile tickling the corner of his mouth. The boy's cola-coloured eyes sparkle, registering my absurdity: my static-grey skin and yellow pipe-cleaner curls bursting wildly from the top of my head. My lolling red felt tongue. My eyes, one round, flat, and green and placed half an inch lower than the left, which is smaller and black and not flat but domed, like half a gumdrop. Me, a handmade toy perched dumbly on the hand of a frazzled and frizzy-haired middle-aged woman—a woman who would look a lot more pulled together, even pretty, if she'd put on a little lip gloss and massaged some serum through her hair like I suggested. She had been going to meet her grandbaby for the first time, and while the baby wouldn't have cared how she looked, her daughter did. Roya would have cared if she made the effort. And Roya had cared, a lot.

I see me as the boy must: a crudely made toy. I admit my appearance is more primitive than Minoo's later creations, but my simplicity has served me well: out of all of us, I'm the only one still here. The boy stands under his rainbow balloon umbrella, smiling. He's the last thing I see before the elevator doors close and Minoo slams me into the steel panel. Slams me again and again until our bodies vibrate with the force of her pain. Our sadness. Because I may be the stuff of stuffing and nonsense, but I can feel as much as Minoo. And of course, I'm the reason Roya shouted at us to leave.

"Leave now and take that thing with you!"

She called me a thing, but Roya knows my name. She could recognize my face before she recognized her own. She's known it almost as long as she's known Minoo's, though I don't claim she's studied mine with as much devotion. Mothers are gods. First true loves.

Minoo falls forward, chest heaving. She rests her head beside mine on the panel. The cool shock of steel is calming, and her breathing slows. My body relaxes. She rolls her forehead so her eyes meet mine.

"It's okay, Minoo." My voice, which has always been high, is tight now too. I clear my throat and try to relax my pitch. "It'll be okay. Let's talk."

THINKING ABOUT MOTHERHOOD: THAT SWEET, DENSE CRUSH

Let's talk about the things you don't want to talk about. Let's talk when you don't want to, when you're afraid. When you're out of words, or the words are razors in your mouth. You don't even have to push a button yet—the elevator can stay here with us, suspended for a moment longer.

Minoo, I'm here. So, let's talk about our mothers.

You remember the afternoon your mother picked you up from school to take you to a doctor's appointment. Or maybe it was the dentist. Or perhaps it wasn't from school at all. She could have been picking you up from a neighbour's or a friend's house. The where-from doesn't matter. It's the where-to that does, because you remember you were happy to see her, your mother. Her creamy hands and frizzy halo of dark hair. The sweet, dense crush of her perfume.

You remember her hands reaching across the back seat to buckle you in, straining over a bag brimming with pomegranates, peaches, and figs from the market. You remember how her teeth were bared in what you thought was a smile. You smiled back, and when you did, you noticed she wasn't looking into your face the way you were pouring yourself into hers. Her eyes were scrunched and walnut-hard and her smile wasn't really a smile at all. Your mother was rooting around blindly, trying to slide the buckle into the slot on the other side of your body and her teeth were showing because she was clenching them. Her lips pulled back, rubber-band tight.

It was then. That was the first time you understood that you wouldn't always make your mother happy, as she always made you happy. That you weren't ever going to be enough.

Let's talk about how our mothers are gods.

All-knowing but unknowable.

In a sense, you, Minoo, are mine. Though when I say *god,* I mean it more in the creator sense of the concept. The distance that exists between mythical or religious deities and their subjects doesn't exist between us. When I say you created me, we both know it is not a figure of speech. You were there the day I was pieced together from felt and wool and wire. You gave me voice. And when I say you live in me, I am not being metaphorical: I mean it. I mean that the bones of your fingers, of your right hand, make up my insides. I mean I feel your skin against the warm, dark confines of my being. The purr of our completeness, it fills me.

But, Minoo, I am not devoid of autonomy. You don't always know what I'm going to do or say until it happens. And if you do know, it's the kind of knowing that's a by-product of familiarity, not control. Like how I know your right pinky finger twitches when you're excited. I know this because I've seen it—I've felt it—a hundred times before. Most recently, not even an hour ago, when we walked down the hall to see Roya, to meet her baby for the first time.

Don't wince. It's okay, you can say it: her baby. Your granddaughter.

Lift your head off the wall and look at me. You don't feel like you deserve to say those words but whether you do or don't is irrelevant. She is your granddaughter. You, her grandmother. Madar bozorg. Yes, in Farsi it feels more natural, the language of your childhood coating the words in halcyon dust. Madar bozorg. It's what you are to her. Anyway, you'd think you'd understand by now that having children—having grandchildren—has nothing to do with deserving them. Children are born and we're automatically undeserving. But we can become otherwise.

Some people do.

Think back: Roya in the hospital bed. Focus on her. Let your eyes drift over the blurry form of Charlie, Roya's partner, pulling his cap down over his eyes. Don't get caught up thinking of how you should probably make an effort to know him better. How it wouldn't be that hard, him being the big floppy-haired puppy that he is, his eyes a friendly wet nose, waiting to nuzzle. It makes sense Roya would gravitate to that complete devotion. That ready affection. I'm not saying you're not affectionate—your body has always been there for her: a mouth for kisses, a warm hand to hold. But who's been on the end of your other hand?

Unscrew your face, I'll get to the point. Think back, and don't focus on the midwife searching through her bag out of actual necessity or just the need to escape the awkwardness of the situation. Scan right past Atanas, who said nothing. Did nothing. Because what was he to do? He's Roya's father, not only your husband, and after all, after everything that brought us to this moment, are you going to tell me you think a parent should pick sides? Should let the love they have for their spouse stop them from doing the right thing for their child? Come on now. We know better. We can't blame him. No one wanted me there, but everyone wanted you, so keep moving with me and ignore all that static, even the bundle held to your daughter's chest—which you can't touch but can feel, its wet new-life heat pressed against your own chest—and home in on your daughter's face: her craggy, beautiful face. The whites of her eyes like glass, her bottom lip quivering like it used to when she was a child on the verge. On the verge of tears. On the verge of mastering herself. That balance, a tension you can feel in your toes. Minoo, azizam—remember how, even then, with her pudgy hands squeezed into fists at her sides, your daughter always tried so hard to stay in control. Because you weren't. Roya had to learn early the same lesson you did: our mothers aren't always who we want them to be. But that doesn't mean they don't love us. It doesn't mean we shouldn't try to love them anyway. I shouldn't have to tell you this. Roya is upset because she loves you so much.

Minoo, take a deep breath. Now ask yourself: Were you who your mother wanted?

You're right, we should go. Press the button then. Ground floor.

Listen, I know it feels like you're falling apart right now, but you're not: you've been unraveling for years. I mean, look at you: curls as big as mattress springs, totally unkempt. Buttons in the wrong holes of your shirt. And is that dried yogurt crusted on your jeans? Look at me. The very fact of my existence. Think of home, your bookshelves and cabinets and dressers that for years were cluttered with dozens of socks like me, our blank button eyes sparkling. Now try to see them with new eyes: how they loomed, pulled over their empty cola bottles, emptiness on emptiness. Ridiculous, isn't it?

Yes, joonam, it's okay to smile. It is ridiculous to think your pain was ever hidden.

Let's talk. Let's talk about how we force our mothers to be gods, and then blame them for failing us. Again, and again.

THERE ARE NO LOOSE ENDS; ONLY OUTCOMES WE DON'T LIKE

Minoo's mother took her to Gilan in the summer of 1992. The province hugged the southwest shores of the Caspian Sea in northern Iran and was home to Parvin, one of her mother's best friends from her school days. Parvin lived in Talesh County with her fifteen-year-old son, Darius, an infant daughter whose name Minoo can't recall, and a husband who Minoo only encountered signs of around the house—an ashtray of freshly crushed cigarette butts, embers scattered and smoldering, the urgent wallop of Kouros aftershave in the bathroom each morning, a pair of worn brown loafers at the back door—but Minoo does not recall ever actually meeting him. Though she must have. She's aware that in the three months she spent at that house, she must have met him at least once. But in the absence of a credible memory, in her mind, he's taken on the form of Freddie Mercury: abundant mustache, elfin overbite, lithe form, and always just leaving the room.

She remembers clearly what was intangible. This is what I'm trying to say. Minoo had never heard of Freddie Mercury until she moved here, to Canada. Until she met Kit at the Immigrant Welcome Centre, and Kit—with her baby-elephant eyelashes and her gentle, clipped way of speaking, as if she were holding in some big secret—turned up the car radio and sang.

How she took Minoo's hand in hers and held tight. But that was a different summer…

Not the summer in Gilan, with the ephemeral husband.

With the bombination of bees around the cherry tree in the garden and a humming radiance that began in Minoo's limbs and blossomed from her chest, freely. It's what she remembers most, even though she knows—she's been told—there are far more important things she should have remembered. There were far more serious matters at hand, if only she could be serious for one moment.

Minoo was slouched on her bed, sucking on the end of her thick braid, when her mother stormed into the room and slapped the hair out of her mouth. Spit flew and splattered against the wall. Minoo's cheek burned and when she touched the heat with the cool tips of her fingers, she smiled: the relief. The thrill of that comfort.

"How did it happen?" her mother demanded to know. "Stop smiling like a donkey and explain yourself!"

But at the time, Minoo couldn't, the explanation being rooted in her body and her body being as it had always been: a distant, devious entity she was reluctantly, constantly, tied to. Mere hours earlier that day, her mother had reminded her that her body was offensive.

"I don't care how hot it is. Cover your forearms, Minoo."

"A bottom like that—like two big balls of dough! It's indecent for your age! At any age!"

And a few weeks before that night, that slap, shortly after they'd arrived in Gilan, Minoo's period had materialized, and her mother had been dumbfounded to learn her daughter hadn't brought any sanitary supplies.

"How does this happen?" her mother snapped, digging to the bottom of her own still unpacked suitcase for the box of pads she had remembered to bring. Her mother's pads were wrapped in purple and looked thicker. When Minoo slipped one into her underwear, she felt like she had a sandwich between her legs. Hungry chuchul, she'd thought to herself and tittered as she walked through the kitchen to the backyard, and her mother, who was in the kitchen, and who never seemed to be far enough away to miss an opportunity to disapprove, furrowed her brows and tsked at the unknown, but undoubtedly, inappropriate source of Minoo's mirth.

So, how does this happen? This is a serious question, hungry chuchuls aside. How did Minoo not realize she was going to have a period while she was away for an entire summer? She had started menstruating the year before, so she should have known it was coming, and yes, she would have if she'd paid attention to such things. But recall, her body wasn't something that bore attention. Her period arrived every so often, and she didn't concern herself with the where or why, remembering what her mother said the night she had gotten her first: menstruation may be natural, but that didn't stop it from being vulgar.

"Aa-miane, Minoo," her mother whispered to her in the darkness of Minoo's bedroom that night, sucking air between her teeth. "Couldn't you have waited for your father to leave in the morning?"

The way she'd stripped Minoo's bed and rolled her sheets, underwear, and pajama bottoms into a tight bundle, her teeth bared in her smileless smile, nose twitching, alerted Minoo to the fact that she—the *she* still standing there, bare-bottomed and backed into the window, head and shoulders silhouetted by the streetlight as a sticky warmth dripped down her legs—was made invisible by the inconvenience of her body.

"Borro," her mother said without looking up. "Clean yourself."

In the morning, after her father left for work, her mother took Minoo to the bathroom and showed her how to conceal her pad with the wrapper of the next napkin before putting it in the garbage.

"If it's very bloody, wrap it in toilet paper too. Do you understand?"

Minoo nodded. Her mother sighed, and for a brief moment, her eyes pooled. It only took that moment for Minoo's mind to splinter with a memory: her mother singing, taking Minoo's small hands in hers and clapping them together.

Atal matal tootoole!
Govee Hasan che joore?
Na shir dare na pestoon!
Shiresho bordan hendestoon…

A silly nursery rhyme. Her mother pressing Minoo's still baby-fat palm against her own cheeks and cooing the nonsense words to her. Giggling. Once, they'd giggled together.

Atal matal tootoole!
How is Hasan's cow?
It has neither milk nor breast!
Its milk is shipped to India…

Minoo could still remember her mother singing, the trill of her own small voice joining in. They sang as they walked through the market. As they tended the roses in the courtyard. The roses her mother loved because, she said, "They are beautiful, but they also know how to protect themselves." She pointed to a thorn. Minoo raised her tiny fists and widened her stance, in her childish approximation of a fighting stance. Minoo's mother laughed lightly, then guided her daughter's hands back down to her sides.

"No, jigaram," she said. "Girls are not the same as roses. Roses naturally grow thorns. Girls don't. We are forced to grow those, as we get older, but it's not natural. Mifahmi?"

Minoo nodded yes, even though she didn't understand at all. What she knew was her elation at the appearance of her mother's dimples, crescent moons carved into her cheeks, and how when her mother laughed, she often pressed her mouth into one of her shoulders, like she was trying to stifle her joy. Minoo wanted to take her mother's face in her hands and lift it to the sun, let her laughter fill the sky.

Minoo couldn't remember the sound of her mother's laughter anymore. It grew small as Minoo grew big.

"Minoo!" her mother barked, bringing her back into the bathroom. "Do you understand? If it is too bloody, wrap it in toilet paper!" Minoo nodded. Nodded at the small garbage bin with tiny pink flowers on it. The oily black of her mother's pupils dilating. Minoo nodded and kept nodding. "No one," her mother repeated, "should be able to tell." Her mother took Minoo's head between her hands and brought its bobbing to stillness. She held her daughter's gaze for a moment longer and moved as if to touch Minoo's cheek. Instead, she pulled her in for a brief, spine-crushing embrace, and then pushed her away.

"Now go to school."

That summer in Gilan, when Minoo's mother asked, and kept asking, "How Minoo, how did this happen?", all Minoo could do was shrug, which her mother saw as insolence rather than the ignorance it really was. She had no idea how it happened. She couldn't tell.

What she knew was this: One evening, Darius found her in the back garden reclined against the gnarled trunk of their medlar tree, her legs stretched out and fanned wide. The day had been hot, and her body was a pummelled mound of clay.

They'd gone to the beach: Minoo's mother and Parvin and Parvin's baby, who Minoo can only remember as a crease in a chubby thigh, a delicate gold chain resting in a fold of supple baby wrist. A flicker memory. A fragment. Minoo relaxed on the sand with her arm thrown over her eyes and felt the light soaking through her skin. Into her blood. And as this warmth spread, so too did a giddy indifference. Minoo could tune out the baby shrieking when her mother stopped her from eating sand, and her own mother's jibes at what other women were wearing. (Not enough of this. Too much of that. They should have stayed at home and been spared this vulgarity.) Could walk into the water to cool off and barely register the whispered criticisms of her body.

"Get ready for when your daughter grows up, Parvin. These girls—bodies unruly as weeds."

Minoo's mother wasn't deeply religious like some other mothers, but the way she saw the world was informed by the conservative religious values she was immersed in growing up. Minoo let the image of her mother scowling on the beach blur in her mind until she'd been erased from the spot of sand she'd occupied on the shore. Minoo floated on her back in the sea, picturing creepers circling her waist, her limbs, curling between her toes and giggling into the dome of blue sky. She pulled back her hijab cap and felt her hair unfurl like tentacles.

"Minoo!" Startled, Minoo lifted her head from the water and found herself in her mother's megalithic shadow. "What are you smiling at?" she barked. "And what are you doing?" Her jaw dropped at seeing Minoo bareheaded. She yanked Minoo's covering back into place, using her hand like a wedge to shove loose tendrils beneath the cap's edge. Minoo felt hair being ripped from her scalp. Felt her eyes water. Wanted to cry out in pain. And still, the laughter kept coming.

"Stop it!" Her mother clapped her hands together in front of Minoo's face. Minoo thought of an angry seal, whiskers bouncing and nose twitching.

"You foolish girl!"

Minoo felt herself being dragged to shore.

"What did I do?" her mother spat, trying to free her stride from her long, clinging swim skirt. "What did I do to deserve such a disgraceful girl?" Her mother stumbled, falling to her hands and knees in the shallows.

Minoo had grabbed her belly to try to stop it, but laughter unfurled, feral and golden. And later that day, that wild and aimless feeling muddled in her bones under the dark canopy of the tree.

"I've been looking for you," Darius said, sitting down in front of her. He wrapped his arms around his knees and fixed his large eyes on her. "It's time for dinner." He said this, but didn't get back up. Instead, he handed her a fig from one of the trees in their garden. He put a finger on the tip of her big toe and wiggled it.

She smiled and wiggled her other toes in response.

He'd been looking for her. She repeated this thought to herself. And when he spoke those words, there was none of the exasperation she was accustomed to hearing. Her wandering self, always a loose end that had to be wrapped up.

Beneath the medlar tree's contorted limbs was her favourite place to be—sheltered and far enough from the house so as not to be entirely visible, but not inaccessible. She could not be accused of hiding: one of her mother's favourite criticisms.

That evening, Darius sat there and smiled back at her, beautifully slack in his own skin. She wanted to slip inside his body—the slickness and sinew; slip inside and see how it felt. She had no idea how things worked when bodies came together, but at least her mother's next question, "Why?", was easier to answer.

Because when Darius looked at her, she didn't feel like he wished she was someone else.

FOR WHAT IT'S WORTH...

When Minoo was sent to live in Ontario—when she was sent away, which would happen four months after the baby was born—Cala, a cousin of Minoo's father, agreed to take Minoo in, sight unseen, person unknown. Relatively unknown, because Cala knew one thing. The very thing Minoo's parents were trying to hide from everyone else. Her parents told Cala the truth about this, her mother said, so Cala would know what a loose, unruly girl she was allowing into her home and could prepare herself. Minoo's dad simply said, "I think you'll like her," and he said this so quietly, locking eyes with Minoo so intensely, for one moment, that Minoo felt that he saw her. That she mattered and might even be able to stay, please. But almost as quickly as her father's eyes met hers, they slipped back behind the newspaper he was reading, so Minoo chewed the insides of her lips and said nothing.

The first time Minoo saw Cala, the woman was in a swarm of security guards at the arrivals gate of Pearson International Airport, looming over a man on the floor, whom she was hitting over the head with a crumpled placard. Mere minutes later, Minoo would notice her own name written on the glossy white poster board in thick black marker with a red heart around it, but at the time, when she walked out into the brightly lit airport foyer, all Minoo noticed was the woman in quilted paisley overalls and thick-soled black boots. She swung the placard, hitting the man again and again. The man, it turned out, had bolted at customs, slid through the glass doors at arrivals, jumped the metal dividers and collided with Cala, who'd been waiting with a sign and flowers for Minoo.

Minoo, who had been dragging her suitcase from the baggage carousel, was vaguely aware of this man as a dark blur streaking past her, in her peripheral vision, and then the security guards as more dark blurs following. Shouting, the words indistinct. She remembered the collective stir of her fellow passengers, voices raised slightly but still sleepily. A subdued murmur. It had been a long trip. Over twenty hours. Everyone seemed like Minoo: too tired to muster shock or curiosity. It was either too late or too early. Eleven p.m. in Toronto. Six-thirty a.m. at home in Tehran. Her son would be waking up. Unbidden, the image of his face came to mind: his ovation of dark eyelashes, and his dimpled smile—he always woke up smiling. She batted away the memory; inhaled deeply against the clawing in her chest. She hauled her suitcase off the luggage carousel and wheeled it behind her out into arrivals. That's when she heard the commotion: a *whap whap whap* and a voice—"You asshole! Khar kosdeh madar jendeh!"

On the floor, the man cowered and covered his head. Cala, flushed and righteous, her long marigold hair flying around in a glorious fury, stood over him. Minoo sucked air deeply into her lungs, remembering to breathe.

"He slammed right into me," Cala exclaimed after the security guards rescued the man and led him away. She was a little breathless and brushing her hair from her still-flushed face. "Right into me! And he crushed your flowers! Oh, azizam, I'm so sorry!" She gestured to the yellow rose petals littering the ground around them, to the poster she was still holding. "Our first meeting—he ruined it." She sucked her teeth. "Kosh kesh." Cala hooked her arm through Minoo's and started walking them out of the terminal. Minoo dragged her suitcase behind her. When they passed a garbage can, Cala stopped and folded the poster board in half.

"Drugs, probably," Cala said. She giggled, a sound that made Minoo think of sparkling tea glasses in a dish rack, drying in the sun. "I hope they were worth it."

"Did you see how the security guards were trying to protect him from me?" Cala slid the poster into the trash. "That'll teach him to ruin someone's perfect moment." They walked a few more steps and then Cala stopped again, abruptly, and turned to Minoo. Minoo's suitcase bumped into her heels. "You've already been through so much, joonam." Cala squeezed Minoo's shoulders. "I'm not sure how I can help you, but I will help you, okay?" Cala hugged her gently. "You and me." She pulled back and rubbed Minoo's arms. "I promise." Cala's face, as she made that promise, looked like a crumpled note, a secret letter. The colour of her eyes was a sweet and familiar fig brown.

Minoo believed her.

"Good." Cala took her arm again to lead them both out into the warm June night; into the fumy perfume of vehicle exhaust, the clean expanse of concrete, and a great black belly of sky.

IN THE HOSPITAL PARKING LOT, THE MEMORIES ARE IMMENSE, AND MUDDLED

Minoo is clutching the steering wheel with her free hand. It's hot, and the steering wheel must be scalding because the air in the car is so stifling that I can feel the very fibres of my being shrink.

"Minoo," I begin.

She starts the car and rolls down a window. The air is still oppressive, but instantly a little less so.

I turn to Minoo, my nose inches from the small chicken-pox scar near her left ear.

"Minoo," I say again. She shakes her head. She's not ready to talk. She needs to think.

Looking back, it seems like the days were sugared with her mother's laughter and then not. But it can't actually be this way. Minoo knows this. She knows her mother didn't suddenly stop laughing, but memory is funny with details. It can be microscopically precise. Minoo recalls being quite young, quite small, sitting on the embroidered stool in front of her mother's dressing table. A blue hyacinth towered in the muted morning light, its thick scent coating the back of Minoo's throat. In this memory, she can see her pudgy, round knees in new white stockings; can feel the lace hem of her dress under her fingers, the slight rock of her body as her feet swing under her bottom. And her mother. Minoo knew her mother was beautiful, and not only in the way all children think their mothers are beautiful. Minoo saw the way people reacted when her mother entered a room. Her mother's face: sweeping cheekbones, arachnid lashes and lips that always looked like she'd just sucked the juice from a sweet, dark plum. Minoo had once used her mom's lipstick to try to achieve the same look, but her mouth only looked bruised, busted. Her mother had all this beauty, but when Minoo thinks of it, she feels cold. Her mother would turn the force of her beauty on strangers, appraising them with such cool disdain they'd look down. Look away. Hang the smiles that had sprung to their faces. As Minoo got older, her mother turned that same look on her. She'd wonder if something could be truly beautiful if nothing good came of it.

But when she was a young child, Minoo was still able to catch her mother's eye in the mirror in time for a wink. Her mother would still brush out Minoo's sleep-matted hair, gently. It was so gentle, you see, and this is what breaks her heart. How her mother had loved her once. Uncomplicatedly.

Then there are other memories, immense, but muddled.

Like the first time she'd held her son. Details of this moment are scarce. She can't recall his newborn squint or tiny fists. But she can recall bright lights, the slurp of her insides as he slipped from her. The humming warmth of his still wet body on her chest. Her mother standing in the corner, her lips set in a thin line.

Both memories have been preserved for a reason. The same reason, really. In these moments, Minoo felt loved. There is nothing so complicated about that, but she has tried to tell me no, it's not about love. It's something else: these moments marked the end of something. By immensity or intensity, she recalls her mother's gentle hands and her son's fetal heat because something bad followed these memories.

This doesn't disprove my theory. Memories of lightness persist because of the darkness that surrounds them.

A seagull drops onto the hood of our car and hops to the windshield where it cocks its head and stares at us, its caviar eyes like mine, unblinking. I cock my head in response, my tongue dangling out of the side of my mouth. We stay locked like this for a few moments, until a dusty red van backs into the parking spot in front of us. The shrieks of children are audible even with the van doors closed. Abruptly, the bird breaks our gaze and capers the distance to the edge of our hood. There, it waits until a door finally slams open and four bickering kids spill from the vehicle's insides, remnants of snacks falling from their clothing.

Clever bird.

As soon as the children are ushered toward the hospital entrance, the seagull floats over to the feast.

I turn back to Minoo. "This isn't that bad you know." Minoo rolls up the window. "I'm just saying, we can work this out. Sure, there are elements of tragedy in this situation and yes, Roya is miffed but we'll figure out how to fix it."

Roya showed up five months ago to let Minoo and Atanas know she was pregnant. It was her first time home in three years. She surveyed the entire main floor from the entryway, her large eyes brimming with contempt, and coolly informed Minoo she had to stop acting like a lunatic—she nodded in my direction—or never see her grandchild. Charlie shifted uncomfortably behind her and shared a pained look with Atanas, who stood beside us, before both men dropped their eyes to their feet.

People talk about moments like this. They say the air was sucked from the room. But that's not what happened. It was the opposite: the air, currents of it, flooded the house and Minoo braced herself, her toes gripping the creaky hardwood floor, her diaphragm driven into her heart. The force of those words—while not spoken forcefully—had the pressure of time behind them. Years spent waiting for release. For courage.

Minoo's fingers fluttered in my skull. Roya was a brave girl. Always had been. We both thought so.

And, Roya continued, she and Charlie would never be married. Charlie didn't care about marriage. His parents were never married. And she didn't see a point.

The point was the way she had looked at her parents when she said that. The level stare, a challenge to them: Tell me how you think you inspired faith in the institution? Minoo didn't mind, though, that Roya and Charlie weren't getting married. Minoo often talked to me about marriage, and she agreed with her daughter: What is the point? Marriage had always seemed to signify more to others than herself. Marriage meant: Good, now you're someone else's problem.

Good, now you're contained.

Good, now you're controlled.

Not that Atanas had ever made her feel controlled or contained. But by the very act of being attached to him in this way—this man, in this institution—people expected Minoo to be a certain kind of a person. Though Minoo doesn't know who she is exactly, she has always known who she is not. While Minoo knows life isn't always good or fair, she also knows it is lined with pockets of joy, and if she closed herself to where or what or how or with whom she found them, she wouldn't be able to go on.

Everyone always wants you to be one thing or the other, don't they?

Good for you, Minoo had wanted to say to her daughter. *Don't get married! Don't have a baby shower! Do whatever you want!* But she didn't say any of this because she suspected Roya needed her defiance as fuel.

Because of that levelling look.

Minoo knew it well. The first time she'd seen it was when Roya was very young. In grade one or maybe grade two—an age where Roya's socks were a little too small to fit over Minoo's hand but slid easily over Roya's own. An age where Roya, like many young girls, idolized her mother and wanted to be just like her. Which meant she wanted a puppet like me. So together, she and Minoo had made one: the same yellow pipe-cleaner curls and button eyes. The same floppy red tongue. Minoo had even bought a pair of small cabin socks, and dissolved the pairing to create Roya's puppet, whom Roya named, in the ingeniously simple naming fashion of children everywhere, Sockie. Roya was delighted with Sockie until the moment she pulled her over her hand and Sockie did not speak.

"Speak, Sockie!" I encouraged. But the puppet remained silent. Roya frowned. "Maybe you need to help Sockie find the words." I suggested, but Roya shook her head. "No."

"Your mom had to help me," I offered. Roya squinted her eyes, as if she saw this statement for the lie that it was. Minoo, of course, hadn't helped me at all. I spoke right away, no urging needed.

"No," she said again. Still, Minoo felt hopeful a connection would form when Roya took Sockie to school with her the next morning, not on her hand, but tucked into her backpack. Sockie never came home.

"I lost it," was all Roya said.

Minoo offered to make her another.

"No."

"Are you sure? Maybe this one will speak." I offered.

That levelling stare.

Maybe all parents want their kids to be like them more than they want to admit.

An infestation. That's what Roya called us the day she walked into the house belly-first with an uncomfortable Charlie in tow. It was a fair description, if you understood that not all infestations are immediately visible. Sometimes you have to lift a mat. Open a cupboard. Shine a light into a dark corner. Look up or under. We weren't exactly everywhere, and if you weren't looking for us, you probably wouldn't even notice our existence. At first. But out of the corner of your eye, you might catch a flash of metallic tulle, a slack-jawed rictus, a googly-eyed wink, and then you'd turn and see one of us, staring back, as if we'd been waiting for you to notice. Then, you'd start looking. Then, you'd start to see we were just about everywhere.

Infestation. She wasn't wrong, and while I was proud of her incisive observation, I was also stung, still feeling the freshness of her affectionate childhood self in my fibres—our adventures beneath the pale green shade of the backyard trees; in the cozy lamp-lit reading nook under the old, creaky stairs. This sting knocked me out of myself enough to see things as Roya might. Dusty socks at every turn, drooping their absurdity. I could even see myself, perched on the windowsill behind the kitchen sink, the bottle of lemon dish soap glowing impossibly electric beside me, red roses peeking around the lattice. The impotent dangle of my red tongue.

"You're addicted to that stupid sock!"

I observed Roya as she stood in the large entryway, chin lifted a fraction beyond haughtiness, toward caution, the studied hardness of her eyes and the round ball of her belly. I loved the girl in that moment, as much as ever; as much as any self she'd ever been or ever would be. Roya wanted me gone and had for years.

When I am trying to justify my continued existence—when Minoo is trying to justify it—we'll say things like, "Well, Roya only started voicing her displeasure in the last few years," which is true but also not the truth. True because Roya never explicitly said she didn't like me until she was more or less an adult. Not the truth, because we both know she'd grown wary of me well before then. You don't need to say something for it to be communicated.

When Roya was still sleeping every night burrowed in a soft mound of beloved stuffies and fluffy pillows, for instance. Let's go back there. Roya's bedroom at night was bathed in the cosmic purple of a lava lamp. Roya was young enough that the queen bed, which was Minoo's when she first moved in with Cala, dwarfed her. Buried there, Roya would peek out from the fluff and softness: a small, smiley, cherub-cheeked child. Many nights, when Roya didn't fall asleep right away, Minoo would join her there, burrowing into the cave her daughter had created. She'd wrap Roya in her arms and feel her daughter's hummingbird heartbeat against the cage of her ribs. They'd pretend the bed was floating in a warm bubble in the middle of the universe. They'd talk about what they saw: comets, stars, planets, the gut-dropping thrill of darkness and snuggly comfort of each other. It was here they'd most often talk of Davood. Roya was never denied knowledge of her brother's existence, and knew about him from the time she could conceive of the notion. Minoo told her about his beetle-black eyes and how much he loved stories, just like her. She told her of how Minoo had him when she was very young, and couldn't care for him on her own, and how she came to Canada for a life where she could be freer. One day, he'd join them here. She kissed Roya's neck and told her of how, just like her brother, her neck was the sweetest place to kiss. Roya would giggle and snuggle in deeper.

Deep-space snuggles—that's what Roya called these moments, and while she never said I wasn't invited, we knew I wasn't.

"Just you and me, right?" Roya would say, standing in the kitchen in her pajamas, waiting for Minoo to finish unloading the dishwasher or make Roya's school lunch or whatever nightly kitchen ritual she was engaged in. Roya wouldn't look at me when she said this; she kept her eyes trained on her mother and her arms wrapped around whatever stuffy she was clutching and her breath held with such intensity. My head hung dumbly down, willing myself into vapor.

Minoo nodded. Just the two of them.

It's amazing to think of how Roya could sense, even then, even young as she was, that something was pulling her mother away. It's amazing how she pushed for these moments alone with her mother. And because the memories of these times exist, Roya has a better vantage from which to be disappointed.

How could I resent her for this? I may not be a bottle of amber liquid or an endless line of white powder, but she thinks of me as a problem Minoo has, an addiction maybe. Yet addiction lacks imagination; it is only focused on its own survival. I admit I may have lost my way, silly thing that I am, wonky-eyed and frizzy-faced. I may have lost the way for Minoo too. It's so easy to do, because every time you try to make sense of life, you stop it from happening. I'm here so life doesn't stop for Minoo. That's all.

I was created to help, and Roya, who stood in front of us that day in the foyer, grown up with a thick curtain of coppery bangs skimming her lashes, and large, wilted green eyes: she's not the enemy.

She's the everything.

Minoo turns on the car's AC full blast and and aims a vent toward my face.

"Was it your mother, maybe, who showed you what happens when you use tragedy as currency?" I ask, tilting my head back and letting the air cool my neck. "When trauma is mined and sold like gold?"

I turn my face from side to side in the now icy blast. Out of the corner of my eye, I notice Minoo begins to do the same. After a moment more in silence, I continue. "So much prostituting our sorrows, to see who has more."

Minoo lets a small smile slip, and I can envision the fantasy she's conjured: her mother on a dark street corner, her bosom spilling immodestly over a dingy corset, competing with other old-timey streetwalkers for the title of Most Disgraced Mother in front of a rowdy crowd of people with fistfuls of sweaty cash.

My daughter stole from her grandparents!

That's nothing, Minoo's mom says, thrusting her chest forward. *Did your daughter get pregnant when she was fourteen and need to be shipped halfway around the world to avoid humiliating her family? Khoda komakam kone!*

We laugh, and I nestle under her chin. "Maybe yours isn't a story of the 'things that won't kill you but make you stronger.' Maybe it's just a story of the things that make you who you are."

I wasn't Minoo's first.

It began with shadows. Teenage Minoo and her baby lying on their backs on the bed, Minoo making shapes with her hands that turned the darkness on the wall into ducks and elephants and butterflies.

Baby, with belly laughter that jeweled the air around them. Baby with his squiggles and squeaks and legs replete with rolls of fat. His chubby fistfuls of Minoo's hair as she leaned over him to kiss his cheeks. Kissed the soft and vital space above his navel that had not yet fused together.

Baby, with scarab eyes that followed the flit of Minoo's long, tapered fingers to the figures on the wall, his face a new world she thought she had a lifetime to explore.

Minoo's mother at the bedroom door, arms crossed, frowning.

It's overwhelming, the power and helplessness at the core of creation. How you can control so much. How you control so little.

At the immigrant services centre in Toronto, sitting in a hard orange plastic chair, Minoo watched a woman in a rich emerald hijab sew a green button onto a grey cabin sock. The woman's hands were dry and cracked, her skin thin and spotted, her fingers rounded at the end like light bulbs, but her painted nails were unchipped, molten red. Minoo continued to watch the woman, transfixed, as she sewed on another button, biting the thread between small, stained teeth when she was done. It wasn't until the woman slid her hand inside the sock and turned its face to her that Minoo understood what she'd been creating.

"Hello, girl," the sock said.

Minoo clasped a hand to her mouth. With the other, she reached out and touched the sock's soft head. It leaned into her hand, nestling into her palm, and she remembered, in that moment, the precise weight and warmth of her baby on her hip. She closed her eyes for one, two, three seconds—and when she opened them, the woman's own glistening gaze met hers.

"Here," the woman said, pulling the sock off her hand and offering it to her. "For you."

Minoo studied its now floppy head, the tight stitching that fastened the buttons to its face. The pipe-cleaner curls and limp little tongue. She wiped her eyes and nodded, taking it from the woman and slipping it onto her own hand.

"Didn't your mother ever tell you," I said, my first words. My eyes twinkling their first button blinks of existence. "That crying causes wrinkles?" Minoo felt a grin split her face, something that hadn't happened in months. Minoo's mother used to say that making a joke out of everything was an idiot's bandage for reality. And reality must be faced, at all costs. But I think—woolly-headed as I am—that some people think this because their childhood self is lost to them, or was never allowed to be. They don't know what it was like to live without the knowledge of the inevitable sadness that will inform their lives. They can't see how carrying lightness is the ultimate act of resistance. That silliness. Foolishness. Fiddle-faddle, even. It's a spark of revolution in the darkness. Every titter of it.

Minoo's mother hadn't encouraged her to have friends, and any friends she did have, her mother specified, should have parents who were doctors, lawyers, or engineers—a preference Minoo never understood, considering her mother had married a man who worked in a bank while she didn't work outside the house at all. So Minoo didn't have many friends, and has few memories of childhood friends. There is one memory that Minoo can still conjure in an instant, though she can't remember the friend's name, and her memory of the girl is limited to a single event. Minoo recalls sitting in the back seat of a car, and the friend, buckled beside her, had a long, inky ponytail that curled perfectly into a tight coil at the bottom. A fat red bow was fastened in her smooth hair, and when she talked to Minoo, her fingers moved in furious, graceful murmurations. They were on the way to the science museum for the girl's birthday, and the girl's parents were in the front seats of the car, speaking in low voices and periodically smiling at each other. At one point the father winked at the girl in the rearview mirror. The mother reached back and squeezed the girl's leg.

The girl babbled on, soft-baked into this world of affection as she was, oblivious to the wonder it caused Minoo. When they arrived at the museum, after the father parked the car but before everyone unloaded, the parents leaned over the centre console and kissed. Tenderly, on the lips. It couldn't have lasted more than a moment, but Minoo felt a thrill shoot to her guts; felt heat bloom up her neck, across her face. The girl continued to chatter away. But that kiss was all Minoo could think about, and as they walked through the museum, exploring the exhibits, Minoo watched the parents shyly, transfixed, for another kiss. Another moment of affection.

As far as she knew, her own parents had never kissed. She'd never even seen them hold hands, though she once saw them pressed together at the kitchen counter, both sets of their hands plunged into a large bowl of ground beef, kneading the pungent combination of red meat, shredded onion, and salt for kebab koobideh. It was during Nowruz, and neighbours were coming over for dinner. The walls of the house were sequined in dancing candlelight, which bounced off the mirror, gold coins, and fishbowl on the table that held the sofreh haft-sin: the arrangement of seven symbols of health and good fortune for the new year.

Minoo sat cross-legged under the sofreh, cracking open the handful of pistachios she'd dumped into the organza skirt of her dress, quietly observing her parents. The way their hips bumped into each other, like two boats tethered in the middle of an ocean. The way they looked down at their hands and never at one another. They worked in silence like this for some time, long enough for Minoo to finish eating and shake the last bit of salt and pistachio skin from her skirt, before her mother started digging through the meat frantically, as did her father. After a moment, Minoo realized they were looking for something, but it wasn't until her dad dropped to one knee and offered up something small between two fingers with flourish that Minoo realized what it was: her mother's wedding ring. Her mother snatched it quickly, tsking and swatting at her father with a dish-rag but Minoo could see her mother's face was arranged in the stern mask reserved for when she was trying not to smile.

And Minoo's father. He looked as he always looked. Shy and besotted when he regarded his wife. Dazed and nervous when his eyes stumbled across Minoo. Especially as she grew older. As her shirts pulled across her chest and her mother became increasingly fussed about what she wore, and when, and with who. Minoo would bring him his tea, and he no longer proffered his scratchy cheek for a kiss. She became aware, slowly, that he wasn't looking at her anymore, merely throwing brief, cursory glances toward the general area where he assumed she existed.

Minoo didn't understand that this wasn't how all fathers interacted with their daughters until Roya started growing up too, and Atanas continued to take Roya to the local museum where he worked as manager. He'd still hug her groggy body to him when she shuffled into the kitchen on weekend mornings. They'd still fall asleep on the couch watching T.V., leaning into each other like well-thumbed books on a shelf.

Atanas was there in the hospital room when Roya told us to leave. His form was stacked broad and backlit by the gapping hospital room window. His features were indistinct but indisputable, pushing thick coils of hair back off his forehead. There was no sense of betrayal to muster for his inaction. He knew as well as we did. He'd been there the day Roya came home and made her feelings known.

He'd been there the day she left and did not return for many years. He'd loaded her bags into the car while Minoo dashed around the kitchen, dumping snacks into a tote for the drive: oranges, a bulk bag of raisins, a box of granola bars. I'd watched from the windowsill and thought, that's too much. The university is only three hours away, but Minoo continued to add more food (a bottle of doogh, a handful of fruit leather, a cucumber) and I realized she didn't know what else to do. Roya was leaving and couldn't wait to get away.

So Minoo scurried about, stuffing the bag until it brimmed, while Roya shifted, the nervous black pupils of her eyes feral. I studied her every move, willing her to look at me and maybe smile—see my existence for what it was: harmless fun. Necessary comfort. But she wouldn't look at me.

She wouldn't really look at any of us, by then. And I guess I wasn't so harmless.

Still, I wish I could have said something to her. To both of them. But roosting in the full morning light, I was voiceless, and Roya left quickly, tearing herself from Minoo's arms while Minoo stood there in faded pajamas, hair bursting out of a hectic braid, rocking slightly from the break.

If Roya had returned those many years later expecting her absence to have changed her mother, she would have been correct. But not in the way she'd hoped. Without her steady disapproval curbing Minoo's prolific creations, we ran riot. Scanning her childhood home from the entranceway, Roya saw how our numbers had multiplied. What used to be a few had grown to a few dozen of us, empty-headed on our empty pop bottles, a moronic twinkle in our eyes.

Roya turned on her father, exasperated. "Dad, how could you let it get this bad?!" And Atanas shrugged, sheepish as a schoolboy caught with a pet frog in his desk. You only had to take one look at him to know that's exactly the kind of boy he had been, with his gangly gait, the grappling-hook reach of his ready affection, and his lopsided smile. His boyish self was never far away. It's one of the things I've always liked best about him.

Atanas may have done nothing but, the way I see it, there was nothing he could do.

BECAUSE BOYS SHOULD BE BOYS AND GIRLS SHOULD BE PERFECT

The plan was clear, but sometimes Minoo didn't listen, though she hears well enough. Her mother explained to her how it would play out: They would stay in Gilan until after the baby was born. They'd tell people Minoo's mother was pregnant and ordered on bedrest due to complications. No need to explain further than that. She was almost forty, so people would probably just assume it was something to do with her age, and when it came to broaching the sensitive indignities of age with a woman, people usually didn't bother. So, bedrest and no travel. Minoo's father would come visit more often to support the story and Minoo would stay by her mother's side, to care for her during the difficult pregnancy. She would be schooled from home. Parvin, of course, would say nothing, having almost as much to lose. Almost, because boys are less of a liability than girls. Less, because boys are allowed to be boys and girls are only allowed to be perfect.

Parvin was not as strict as Minoo's mother, and she had no real reason to be. Parvin hadn't been raised by a widow with three older sisters, the youngest of which was older than Minoo's mother by eight years. Sisters who were always making trouble. Drinking, smoking, running about with boys and causing her mother no end of embarrassment.

"The neighbours were always talking about us," Minoo's mother had told her when she was a child. "They could talk about us and point to our disgrace and pretend they had none of their own. It weighed on my mother heavily. I was the only one with her while my older sisters were out spreading their legs to any man who belched in their direction, I saw how it clawed at her heart. They say she died because her heart was weak, but I know. My sisters killed her. That is why you'll have no contact with my family. Jendeh. All of them."

"All of you." Her mother said now, including Minoo, "All of you are whores."

As she whispered these words, sitting with her head bowed at the edge of Minoo's bed at Parvin's house, the effort seemed to exhaust her. Her hand, resting by her thigh on the creased purple bedspread, looked grey. Minoo reached out and placed her cool fingers over her mother's, who sighed and hooked her daughter to her side in what might have been a hug if it hadn't been so hard.

Darius, the mothers agreed, would also stay at the house, though they went back and forth on this decision for a few days. Ultimately, it was decided that sending him away might arouse suspicion. But he and Minoo weren't to be together unsupervised anymore. "Although," Minoo's mother had said, laughing mirthlessly, "the damage is done." And as cowed as she felt, this snide comment comforted Minoo. It meant that her mother could still recognize humour, even if she expressed it humourlessly. It meant maybe the mother with the crescent dimples and haloed hair and laughter like the water babbling softly in the fountain in the courtyard behind their house might yet exist, somewhere. Dozing in the garden, the drone of bees numbing her brain, Minoo would think of that sound. She'd think of it until she fell asleep and dreamt of her mother and her as goldfish in that fountain: quick, sun-warmed, flashes of light.

For the rest of her time in Gilan, Minoo seldom saw Darius, either by his design or someone else's. She didn't ask, because asking would have expressed interest, and that's something she knew she couldn't show. Her interest had put her in enough trouble. But she caught glimpses of him out her bedroom window, now and then, playing with his baby sister in the front yard—peek-a-boo, pass the ball, and helping her learn to walk, her tubby hands clasping each of Darius's index fingers while he stepped backwards, slowly. If Minoo closed her eyes, she could see them perfectly: Darius's wide, white smile; the back of the baby's head; those ribbon silk curls at the nape of her neck. By the time Minoo left, the baby would be toddling, no help needed. No help wanted. If anyone tried to steady her, she'd shriek and slap them away, her small hands flying as fast as flippers. Minoo loved that about the girl and thought about it often, whenever she allowed herself to think of that time. And every time, she'd smile. The determination in that girl, young as she was.

The two families continued to have meals together; a last vestige of the mothers trying to pretend everything was fine. (And isn't that the way it always is? The adults pretending harder than kids ever do?) Though this too stopped.

One evening after dinner, while Minoo was helping to clear the platters of food, Darius had reached out to touch the ball of her belly. He'd looked up at her, lips parted. A smile. And without thinking—without noticing her mother's daggered look—Minoo smiled back.

They were just children. They were children and they'd played a game; a new game. And like many new games dreamed up by children, the real world lacked the requisite enchantment to sustain it.

The families ate separately after that: Minoo and her mother and father, when he was there, ate early, and then Minoo was ushered off early to bed. Minoo recalled Darius's face when he touched her belly—that electric shock of delight. She closed her eyes and explored the milky cloud of stupefied wonder that filled her body. And as her baby grew, so did the wonder. A quiet nimbus emanating from her body, quivering silver, feathered light. This was not the boisterous, embarrassing, puppy-dog astonishment her mother was expecting from her daughter. The sort she had come to expect. Minoo's mother often liked to remind her of the time her father had returned from visiting Cala in Canada: Cala, who was just a name to Minoo then. A distant relative and a distant land. Cala had sent two wooden marionettes as gifts: one was a Mountie outfitted in a satin-lined, rabbit fur hat, scratchy red jacket, and black jodhpurs. The black-currant eyes gleamed and the mouth painted under the equally black mustache stretched in a thin facsimile of a smile that made Minoo's guts squirm. She liked the second puppet better, an anthropomorphic moose wearing an *I ♥ Toronto* T-shirt and red-and-white sneakers. She found comfort in its dopey grin and the joyous flare of its nostrils. Since Minoo had no interest in the Mountie, her parents offered it as a gift to the young couple next door who were expecting their first child. Minoo watched the couple admire the toy, marvelling at the real satin lining of the hat and the little patent leather boots, and as she watched, she felt their delight ribboning out from them into her. When she told them that the Mountie had been intended for her, but she didn't like it and was so glad it found someone who did, she wasn't being spoiled and rude, as her mother accused her of being later. She was simply, completely, overwhelmed with happiness for them.

This was the Minoo her mother was used to. The Minoo she expected for the duration of the pregnancy: a girl unhinged and unable to exercise discretion. But as Minoo's belly expanded, so did her calm. She became cat-like in her ability to find and monopolize the smallest sun-spot for naps. When open, her eyes fell constantly and contentedly on her stomach. Her fingers drew languid circles on the hard mound. This subdued affection, the unthinkable shift it signified, bothered her mother more than the bubbling and brash antics of the child she thought she knew. So, she reminded Minoo, again and again, of stories like the Mountie and the moose; stories to remind her of how silly and stupid she was. Stories to remind her: You are not good enough to be a mother. This baby will not be your baby. This baby will not be yours. You are not its mother. You cannot be its mother. You are a foolish, foolish child.

A child.

You are my child. These are words Minoo wished she'd heard. *You are my child and that is your child and we belong to each other.* But no such words were spoken. There were only clear divisions. And between those divisions, emptiness.

The baby was born on a Wednesday evening. He came fast for a first child, so there was no time for an epidural, but the doctor allowed Minoo laughing gas, which she held to her face and inhaled until she became less concerned by her awareness of the pain. She was equally less concerned by her mother's scowl. Minoo took another snootful of gas, a smile slipping across her face like a runny egg. *Damage done!* Minoo thought as her body split open. *What's the point of scowling now?*

By the following Wednesday, they were on their way home to Tehran.

THE ORIGINS OF OU

Minoo and I pull out of the hospital parking lot.

"How many hospitals like this are left in the world, do you think?" I'm looking at Minoo as I ask the question, but she's looking ahead and continues to look ahead, gnawing on her bottom lip. I get it: she doesn't want to talk, but something about today has made me nostalgic for the wonder of small-town hospitals on streets choked by the shadows of old maples. The comfort of thinking of hospitals like this in the world, anachronistic as they are. Little hospitals with gift shops that sell powder-pink and blue baby sweaters, hand-knit in Merino wool by the cotton-ball-haired volunteers who smell like talc. I have no knowledge of these details firsthand, of course. I can only imagine them so precisely because Minoo has seen them, and I know what she knows, I see what she sees, sometimes clearer. I can see the packs of gum and mints and candy bars at the gift shop checkout. The teddy bears, and bouquets of fresh cut flowers in vases, and a shelf with toothpastes and brushes and soaps and other travel-size personal hygiene items. Such small, tender considerations to cushion the existence of unimaginable pain in such a place. How thoughtful. How thoughtful and absurd, these gestures.

Atanas told Minoo this hospital was going to close the maternity ward within the next few years. Babies would be born in a hospital fifty kilometres away, in a bigger, neighbouring city, or so Roya had told him. She had shared this bit of information at dinner, a dinner where she and Charlie had also shared their birth plans. Minoo hadn't joined them—not because she didn't want to—but because the restaurant, owned by some friend of Roya's from university, was too far away. And too noisy. Probably. And Minoo didn't like to drive at night. Though she wouldn't have had to drive. Atanas would have driven them both, gladly. And,

and,

and.

Atanas would have loved to have held Minoo's hand, free of me for once, maybe, in the car. I would have liked that for him. I could feel his cool palm pressed against Minoo's; his long fingers threaded through her own. But Minoo was miffed. When Atanas relayed the news of the hospital from Roya, she felt betrayed. She should have known these things; should have been the one discussing birth plans with her daughter.

"But you didn't want to go," I remind her. "You wanted to stay home."

But.

but

but

Minoo has a but for everything these days.

Minoo stops at a red light. I release my grip on the steering wheel to look her in the eyes. They are glass, reflecting myself back to me. I continue where our mind has left off. "I'm just saying you didn't want to go. You can tell yourself it was because of the noise or the drive, but if you'd really wanted to, you would have gone."

She can tell herself she would have gone if the restaurant were in town, which is maybe true, or if Roya had come over for dinner, which is truer, but the fact remains she didn't go because the whole evening—the restaurant, the proximity to Atanas in the silence of the car, the inescapable knowledge that her daughter thinks she's ridiculous, and the reality of having to exist with these truths, without me, who it went without saying was not invited—was unbearable. Just like the reality of those gift shop shelves with neatly folded, delicately stitched baby sweaters, sitting empty. The sweet old ladies who used to make them, disintegrating into a dust-flecked past.

It's funny how in our minds, everything gets caught up in everything else.

Minoo and I stayed home the evening Atanas joined Roya and Charlie for dinner. While they ate and laughed and had a great time, probably, and maybe also felt a little easier without Minoo there, and definitely without me, Minoo puttered around the vegetable garden. I watched her from the window as she weeded, munched on the snap peas, watered. She looked up at me on my window perch from time to time, and her brow would furrow, the fingers of her right hand would twitch. After a meal of bread, cheese, and sun-saturated tomato, Minoo went for tea with Mrs Beswick next door. They sat on her front porch. She and Mrs B had been volunteering at the local community centre a couple of mornings a week for five years, watching the babies and preschoolers while mothers took free yoga or Pilates classes. I admit, it's been nice to be around young children again. Unencumbered by the learned cynicism of older kids and adults, these small people don't question my existence. They delight in the hilarious miracle of it.

"Can I touch him?" one of the children asked the other day. The child had a soft lisp that reminded Minoo of the white foam of a cresting wave. Usually, the child didn't say more than a necessary "yes please" or "no, thank you" when spoken to, so Minoo and I were surprised at the question.

"Oh yes," I said, clearing my throat and leaning my head toward the child. "As long as you promise not to pull on my eyes or hair. I don't like that."

The child gave a shy nod and raised a stout little paw to my face.

"And guess what?" The child explored my woolly nose with a roly-poly finger. "I'm not a him. Or a he, or a she, or a her, necessarily. It's okay that you called me that, though. I could be one of those things or the other. I'm just not."

The child peered over thick-lensed glasses and regarded me frankly.

"But your name is Ecology *Paul*."

"Yes, I can see how that would be confusing. A dear dear friend named me, and the name just kinda stuck! But I don't think of myself as just a he or she."

Are you an *it*?"

I shook my head. "No."

"Then what are you?"

"Well, I guess I'm an *ou*."

"An *ou*?"

"Yes, an *ou*. In Farsi—that's the language people speak where Ms Minoo is from," I tilted my head to Minoo, "There are no different words for he or she, though of course there *are* boys and girls. The language doesn't make a distinction. Everyone is just an *ou*, and that's what I am."

The child stopped stroking my nose.

"Are you from that place too?"

"Iran? Not exactly. But I am from Minoo."

The child squinted, absorbing this information.

"And you are Minoo."

"Yes," I laughed. "So *ou* makes sense, don't you think?"

The child's head bobbed. His petting resumed.

Before leaving for tea with Mrs B that evening, Minoo had regarded me on my bottle behind the sink. She stood considering me for a moment before nodding, as if to say, *See? I don't need to take you everywhere. I go for walks without you. I grocery shop without you. I don't take you with me when I get my oil changed or go to the dentist. It's not because I need you that I didn't go to dinner tonight.* Then she turned on her heel and left, so I couldn't remind her of the power of proximity even if I'd tried. Couldn't have reminded her that the walks are only around the neighbourhood. That when she goes grocery shopping or to the mechanic, I'm usually in the car, tucked into the centre console or glove compartment.

I couldn't have reminded her of how our proximity was a problem and had been for a long time. When Roya was in kindergarten, how she would sob at drop-off time, her doughy hands grabbing for Minoo's shirt, as if being physically separated from her mother would kill her. But that changed as Minoo became more dependent on me. Which happened as she became more lost to herself—a common side effect of motherhood, yes, but also, a side effect of never learning to know yourself in the first place.

Minoo, I would have said. You leaving me here, now, is no great feat. I'm further away from you when you take a bath than I am when you sit not ten feet away sipping peppermint tea with Mrs B. Mrs B wouldn't have batted an eye if Minoo *had* brought me along, knowing me as she has for all these years, from the time Minoo was a teenager and would slip me over her hand to help her run lines for whatever play she was in, or to talk through a difficult day, or sometimes, to simply feel the warmth of a second skin.

But what would have been the point of pointing this out? We dress up this truth-telling as for the benefit of others when really, we only seek to satisfy ourselves.

We hear the police car before we see it: the shrill blip of a warning siren. Blue lights flash in the rearview mirror and our eyes instinctively drop to the speedometer. Not speeding. I turn to face Minoo, who looks at me then back at the road.

The siren blips again.

"Minoo! Pull over!" She bobs her head, acknowledging my words, but keeps driving. "Minoo!"

She throws on the indicator, drifts to the curb, and puts the car in park.

"Maybe I should chill in the centre console," I say. Instead, she shoves me into her lap. "Minoo?" I call from her crotch.

I hear the window rolling down.

"Can I have your licence, insurance, and registration?" The voice reminds me of calf leather. Supple and young.

Minoo isn't moving. "Licence, insurance, and registration, ma'am?"

A whiff of mint drifts into the car. Then I hear it: the wet smack of chewing gum.

"Ma'am?" *Smack, smack.*

I feel the muscles in Minoo's thighs tense. I poke my head up out of Minoo's lap. "Erhem, excuse me, sir." The police officer bends slightly. "I can probably help you with that."

His sunglasses slide down the straight bridge of nose. His lips part.

"Just give me a minute."

Rummaging around the glove compartment, I find the old prescription sunglasses Minoo thought she'd lost but obviously hadn't even looked for, a broken dream-catcher keychain that Roya made years ago, a pair of scissors, dozens of packets of ketchup, a sugar-pink suede glove, and a crumpled map of Eastern Ontario.

"What the fuck," I mutter. I pull myself back out of the compartment and take a deep, steadying breath. Turning to the cop, "Just give me one more sec." I dive back in, rifling out the entire contents of the glove compartment to finally find the small plastic insurance and registration envelope crushed into the back corner.

"Ah ha!" I emerge, triumphant, the envelope stuffed in my mouth. "Here you go, officer," I mumble.

He looks at Minoo. Her mouth is bunched up like a pulled stitch. Slowly he takes the documents I'm holding out the window. He flips open the black envelope and scans the paperwork Then he looks at Minoo. Then me. Then Minoo. He appears on the verge of saying something to her but turns his attention back to me. He takes off his sunglasses. "I still need your… er, I mean her licence, mister…"
"Ecology Paul."

"Mr Paul."

"No, not mister. Just Ecology Paul."

"Okay. Mister… sorry—Ecology Paul."

"Yeah, thanks. I'll look."

I dig around Minoo's purse until I find her wallet, which I grab and hold out to Minoo. Minoo feigns total absorption in the nails on her other hand. Suppressing the urge to throw the wallet at Minoo's head, I drop it in her lap instead and begin searching. She never puts cards in the right place. Most of them aren't in the little card slots, but in the space the bills should be. Or shoved in the spot meant for pictures. I finally find her licence in the change pocket.

As the officer is reviewing her documentation, I wonder how well cops are trained to deal with mental health crises. "It's been a really weird day," I say.

In the bronzed light of afternoon, the officer's irises patina. His eyebrows are so blond they glitter. He raises one of them now and his forehead hardly creases. My God, I realize, he's a child.

I suck my lips into my face. "What I mean is, she's going through something. She's not usually like this."

Minoo and I don't speak during the time it takes for the officer to return to his cruiser to check her information. I stare at her though. I get right up to the side of her face and stare, for all the good it does. Minoo is somewhere else. I feel the dampness of her mind's dulling mist. I know she's sitting tranquil in the midst of it, my warm, woollen weight on her hand, a comfort.

This is hardly the first time I've questioned the nature of this reliance, which is shrinking her, like a cashmere sweater in the dryer, into something unrecognizable. And I know that, if indeed we are created for a purpose, this was never mine.

The police offer returns, nervous energy replaced with a calm command. The convex mirror of his sunglasses, now resting properly again on the bridge of his nose, dispassionately reflects Minoo and me, who stare at him. "Listen," he says, looking pointedly at Minoo and only Minoo. "I only pulled you over because your rear left brake light is out, so your signal isn't working. And I'm not sure what's going on here, with the sock and everything," he gestures vaguely in my direction but still won't look at me, "but I don't want to ticket you. You know, for failing to signal. But

I do need you to promise you'll go straight home from here. Straight home and have some chamomile tea. Watch some TV. Relax or something."

Minoo nods slowly—a little too slowly to be convincing that she was really listening—but I take back the insurance envelope being held out to us before the cop can change his mind. For this reason, I also refrain from thanking him and don't speak again until he's walking back in his cruiser.

"Jesus Christ, Minoo," I say. "That was too ridiculous, even for me." Minoo looks at me for the first time. Seeing me struggle to fix her with the most serious gaze my uneven eyes can muster, she smiles. Smiles as her eyes silver with tears, and a few wiry grey hairs on her otherwise still dark head leap and spiral upward.

"Jesus Christ," I say again, peeking over Minoo's shoulder to make sure the cop is out of earshot. I roll up the window just as she begins to sob. "My poor girl," I purr, curling into her chest. "You're just a mess, aren't you?"

WHY I'M MOST BELOVED

Kit.

I am most beloved because of Kit, which in a sense, is lovely, because that's what Kit was: so lovely.

Which is, in another sense, deflating, because we all want to be loved for ourselves. But I never stood a chance that way, never having a self to begin with.

Kit emigrated with her mother from Norway a month before Minoo arrived in Canada. Minoo met her at a free beginners English lesson her first week at the Immigrant Welcome Centre. They studied together, even though they'd arrived in the country already almost fluent in English. Kit had a raspy voice like scissors cutting through corduroy, wheat-coloured hair, and a square jaw so precise and so vulnerable in this precision, that whenever Minoo saw it, she wanted to press her lips to the bottom corner of mandible. Kit smelled always, simply, of Ivory soap. Sharp and mellow.

Minoo could admit to herself, even then, that she loved Kit. She wanted to be near her all the time. What she could not admit was the nature of that desire. Kit made Minoo think about things she knew she should feel ashamed to think of. But when Kit was near, she didn't think of shame. Kit inhabited the same type of body as her own, with the same curving places, the same fleshy places, the same wet and dark and dirty places. Minoo thought about what her doctor in Tehran had said about her body after the baby: how it would never be the same again, and how when he said this, he'd shook his head and his mouth puckered like a dried fig. Minoo recognized disapproval when she saw it. She remembered that look on her mother's face when, fresh from a shower, she'd danced around the room in her towel, singing along with Googoosh into her hairbrush. Or when she laughed too loud, or spoke before spoken to. Or ran, which made her bits bounce. Or slouched, which made her seem lazy and uninterested in what people were saying to her. Or burped, or left a smell in the bathroom when she was done using it, or smiled at the boy in the market who polished her father's work shoes. And she remembered her mother's look during the weeks after she'd had her baby, when she'd bled and bled, staining her underwear and sheets and towels. How her face compressed, and her features huddled in disdain. Cala had caught Minoo making a similar screwed-up expression one afternoon when she arrived home from the Immigration Centre.

After class, Minoo and Kit would usually hang around the centre and do a craft the organizers laid out for them, or go to the mall for smoothies or frozen yogurt. But that time, in the fit of the summer heatwave, Kit had made plans to go to the outdoor pool with a few of the other students. Minoo had not been intentionally excluded—the plans were made the day before, when Minoo wasn't in class because Cala had surprised her with a trip to Canada's Wonderland. Still, Kit—who was hurriedly throwing her notebook and textbook into her backpack so she could catch the bus to the pool—felt terrible.

Minoo reorganized the contents of her satchel, trying to appear unbothered by the oversight. She spotted me at the bottom of the bag, where I'd been stuffed since the day I first spoke to her weeks ago. She put the workbook she'd been holding down on the table and lifted me out. She began to twist one of my flattened pipe cleaner curls back into shape.

"I'm so sorry," Kit placed her hand on Minoo's forearm. From the doorway, another student called for Kit to hurry up. "Minoo, I'm serious." She swung her bag over her shoulder. "I want you with me. I want to hang out with you. I owe you an ecology Paul tonight."

Minoo looked up. An ecology Paul? Minoo mouthed the words, trying silently to question meaning into them. Kit was halfway to the door before she spun around, realizing what she'd said.

"Apology call, Minoo!" Giggles splashed from her mouth. "I meant I owe you an apology call tonight!" Kit waved over her head and was gone. Minoo slipped me onto her hand. I looked at her and smiled.

Isn't it funny how things that happen by accident can end up making the most sense?

During the bus ride home from the centre, a young woman plopped into the seat directly across from Minoo. She sat there, leaning forward, her eyes shadowed by a ballcap, elbows resting on bare thighs, as she fiddled with her Discman. Her jean cut-offs were short enough that the lining of the inside pocket poked out the hem. Her T-shirt was striped orange and white. It reminded Minoo of the Creamsicles she'd bought with Kit last week. They'd eaten a whole box in the park behind the centre, sitting on the swings.

Minoo licked her lips with the memory.

In the heat, veins bulged from the woman's forearms, and when she sat back and saw Minoo's eyes on her, she smiled; a spritely reflex that drew attention to her upturned nose. She rested her head against the window behind her and closed her eyes. The woman was relaxed, her knees bowing out to the sides and her body melting into the seat. This was a woman who took up as much room as she pleased, and Minoo, who found herself absorbed by the soft flesh of the woman's inner thighs, had to look away quickly.

For the rest of the ride home, Minoo kept her eyes focused out the window in front of the driver. Apartments, condos, and malls gave way to subdivisions, farmland, trees, and eventually, the satellite town where her aunt lived. By the time she got off the bus, Minoo was convinced it was better that she hadn't gone to the pool. The idea of Kit seeing her in a bathing suit made her feel like a too-full water balloon. About to burst, at any moment. As she walked through the front door of her aunt's home, she was sure this feeling of excruciating fullness was worse than Kit's pity.

"What's with the face?" In the kitchen, Cala was standing in front of the open fridge, eating spicy Persian pickles from the jar, briny juice running down her wrist and falling in dark splotches onto the front of her peach silk slip. The abundance of Cala's dyed blonde hair was piled on top of her head and held tenuously in place by a large claw clip. Minoo thought about how her mother would have yelled at Minoo to shut the fridge door; that she was wasting electricity and spoiling the food. But Cala never yelled, and never worried about small expenses if they made someone's life more comfortable. Like if you left the fridge door open for a bit to cool yourself because the day was sweltering. Or if Minoo left the fan running all night, even in the winter, because the hum filled her body and made it easier for her mind to sleep. Cala never minded.

"The face?" Cala asked again, gesturing around her own glistening, flushed face with a dripping pickle. "Looks like you ate something sour."

Minoo fell into a chair, dropping her satchel to the floor. I tumbled out along with her water bottle and pencil case. In her mind, Minoo ran her eyes down the front of Kit's body—the ridges of her clavicle, small breasts the size of pin cushions, the soft mound of flesh between her hips... Minoo was imagining things now. She'd never seen Kit in anything other than T-shirts and jeans or loose-fitting shorts. But she could tell, she was sure, she could make out her curved and soft, cushioned places if she tried.

Minoo's lips bunched up tighter.

"That face! Right there!" Cala pointed the pickle at Minoo and kicked the fridge door shut behind her. "Whatever's causing you that tension, you've got to let it go. Unless you're hiding a body under your bed or something, it's not worth it."

Cala padded across the kitchen to the table. "And even then, it depends on whose body."

Minoo didn't smile. Or even acknowledge Cala's existence. Cala sighed and flopped down on a chair at the table beside Minoo.

"Listen, if you can't tell me whatever's going on, that's fine. But you've got to talk to someone." She spied me sprawled on the floor and picked me up between her toes, her eyebrow raised in quizzical amusement. "Like this guy," she said, handing me to Minoo with her foot. "Talk to him."

SMALL CAGES FOR BIG FEELINGS

Minoo was eight, climbing up the supporting pole of the swing set in the playground at school, the first time she experienced The Tickles. She didn't know what they were, only that the exertion of her climb, the grip of her legs around the rusting metal, caused something to swell and burst inside her.

When it was over, she dropped to the sandy ground and stood there, looking around. The other children were playing, like nothing happened. No one noticed her flushed cheeks, bright eyes, the way she crossed one leg over the other as if she was trying to hold something in.

Minoo didn't talk to anyone about The Tickles the first time they happened. She was a child, and the feeling was all-consuming but amorphous, rooted only in herself and her body. She was a teenager before she attached this feeling to other people; to sexual attraction. And only when she met Atanas would she learn its universal name: an orgasm. She simply called it The Tickles, due to the limits of her vocabulary and how the sensation made her body feel. Vulnerable and excited.

Her mother had certainly never told her what it was called, and, a few months after the first playground experience, Minoo eventually asked her. Looking back, Minoo is amazed by her nonchalance. How she asked this question as easily as she had once asked her mother why skin itches and her mom had answered, "Because it wants attention." And Minoo had smiled to herself, thinking of her skin as a soft, needy animal.

In truth, the reason Minoo was so unburdened by the question of The Tickles was that she hadn't yet learned to depise her body. She didn't know shame or bodily autonomy. Her physical self was still an extension of her mother's will. Her mother bathed her. Made sure she was clean after using the bathroom. Cut her fingers and toenails and brushed her hair. Her mother knew every function and inch of Minoo's body, which is why, one night at dinner, when the rich and fragrant smell of the walnut and pomegranate stew her mother was spooning onto the bed of steaming rice on her father's plate made her mouth water—and when this watering reminded her of the feeling between her legs in the playground—she didn't think anything of asking about the sensation.

Her mother stood there, ladle suspended above the serving bowl. Minoo watched the stew drip, the oily droplets rippling their dinner's velvety brown surface: one, two, three drops before her mother placed the ladle into the bowl and sat down. Minoo wasn't sure if her mother had heard her correctly, so she repeated the question. What was that feeling?

Her mother smoothed the sapphire blue sofreh spread in front of her. Minoo turned to her father, who was determinedly stuffing basil, mint, and onion into his mouth. Her stomach growled as she gazed at her still empty plate.

"Minoo." Her mother's voice was low, like thunder rolling in the distance. "Those are not feelings children should have. Those are adult feelings. Feelings adults have when they are married."

Minoo remembers the feeling of her insides going cold and her hunger vanishing. There was something wrong with her. Something wrong with her body.

"Minoo!" her mother barked. Minoo and her father jerked to attention. "I need you to say you understand," she reached across the sofreh and grabbed Minoo's hand. "Those are bad feelings. You have to stop."

Minoo's eyes dropped to her small hand, caged under her mother's, then lifted to her mother's face, which was contorted with an expression Minoo had never seen but would carry around the memory of for years before she could identify it. The parted lips, flared nostrils, wide eyes: Fear.

Minoo nodded. Yes, she'd stop.

SHE WAS THE PERFECT ALICE

Minoo slows down as we drive by the empty lot where Roya's primary school used to be. Roya attended the school until grade six, which is when kids were bused to a middle school the next town over. Last year, the primary school was demolished. A new, bigger school was built a little further out of town that went up to grade eight, combining kids from several surrounding areas.

Minoo misses the old building. There's not even a dumpster in the lot anymore. Not the smallest piece of rubble. All signs of the school are gone. When the school still stood, it looked like a bicycle wheel from the sky: the hub was a gym, big and round. A hallway wrapped around the gym's perimeter like a track. Classrooms and an office spoked out from this centre. Minoo visited the school plenty of times during the day, dropping off a forgotten lunch or volunteering in Roya's class, but it's the after-hours events Minoo cherished most: the holiday concerts, fundraisers, and end-of-year fairs. The way in the early evening, light bent and then faded through the windows, soft. How Roya and her friends would run around the hallway, round and round, exhilarated to be set loose in a place of rules and restrictions. Minoo can still feel Roya's hand slip from hers; can see her child fly ahead, a thick braid bouncing against her back. In Minoo's mind, Roya turns to smile, which probably never happened. Roya wasn't the sort of kid to look back.

This afternoon as we cruise by the vacant lot, scraggly patches of grass and Queen Anne's lace sprout from the packed dirt, erratic and lonesome.

"What do you think they'll build there?" I ask.

Minoo shrugs and looks straight ahead.

"You're right," I say, "We should think of something else."

The three of us shrouded in a blanket of silver morning: Roya, Minoo, me. Roya was still a baby. She laid on her back and squealed, delighted, mouth open to reveal gurgling darkness.

Minoo stretched out beside her, hair fanning out from her head and I hovered above the pair, telling a story. Minoo had heard it before. The story was hers. It was one of the few stories her father had told her, when he still bothered to tell her anything, about his childhood on his father's cotton farm in Gorgon.

"One day, the workers in the field heard a high-pitched cry and followed the sound to a well. The well was part of a *ghanat*—an ancient Persian underground irrigation system. Can you say *ghanat*, Roya?"

Roya babbled and made a grab for my face. She was fast. I'd already had to have one eye reinforced because of her baby claws, so I move back a little before I continued.

"There, in a well, they found a baby horse. A colt. It had fallen in and was trapped. The workers ran to tell the farmer—Minoo's grandfather—who was a stubborn but kind man. The farmer said they must all go back to the well with ropes to save the colt. But after hours of trying, they could not lift the horse out. The farmer's young son suggested they get the tractor, and using the machine and the workers, they were able to free the baby.

"However, they could not find the mother. The horse was branded with the mark of a Turkoman tribe, but as far as everyone knew, there were no Turkoman people around. So, the son raised the colt, who grew into a fine, strong mare that was treasured and cared for her whole life."

Minoo remembered how her father's eyes would mist over as he told this tale. How every time she asked him to tell it, he'd add more detail or change a detail to make the story different; perpetually exciting.

As I told the story to Roya, I was aware that this was the first of many times I'd tell it, and I dug into my mind for the iterations Minoo had told me. All the iterations her father told her. The one where the Turkoman tribe came for the colt, but seeing how it loved the son, let it stay. Or how they stole the horse, but it ran away, across mountains and miles to return to her beloved and bereaved boy. Or the one where they didn't need ropes or a tractor at all. The colt needed only to see the tears in the boy's eyes to leap out of the well and into the child's arms.

Minoo must have heard dozens of versions before her father stopped telling the story; before her mother intervened and said thirteen was too old to keep entertaining such silliness. Minoo's father did as he was told because it was part of the bargain he'd struck with his wife before they were married—one he was reminded of on this and many other occasions in front of Minoo: if their first child was a girl, it would be their only child. One girl was more trouble than ten boys. And if it was a girl, he would not contradict her in matters concerning upbringing. Since this was nearly all matters, her father's silence was one of the steadiest constants in her life.

I made a promise to Roya then, lying on the floor, giggling, and gurgling, and still trying to grab at my face with her pillowy hands, that I'd tell her the story every time she asked—I'd find a thousand new ways to tell it if I had to. Maybe that was why Minoo's father kept coming up with new versions: to keep his child coming back to him.

Minoo's father loved her as much as he was capable, since loving her mother seemed to demand most of him. Minoo never understood this, but never questioned it either, the way young children often don't question their reality until they become aware of alternative worlds, other possible ways to live.

"Your father was crazy for your mother," Cala said one evening. It was early spring and the windows were open. Birdsong bobbed into the kitchen where Cala and Minoo sat at the kitchen table, tea cooling in pink-tinted tea glasses. Between them, an open box of fresh Medjool dates. This table was the only furniture Cala would take with her when she eventually moved out, leaving the rest to Minoo. Only about the width of an adult's arm span, the table seemed capable of magically accommodating innumerable guests and plates of food when needed. The wood, a delicious dark honey, looked liquid, and the table's legs tapered to elegant ankles and intricately carved clawed feet. But what Minoo loved the most about the table was its top. Cala had covered it in a mosaic of her mother's Meenakari ceramic plates, which had shattered during shipment from Iran. Each piece was not much bigger than a bobbin and contained geometric patterns of deep blue and turquoise, pink, copper, and cream. Cala, always one with an eye for potential, had glued the pieces in place and sealed the final product.

"They were broken," Cala said when Minoo first marvelled at her creation. "And now look!" she beamed, "They're part of something completely different and just as beautiful!"

Waiting for her tea to cool, Minoo ran her fingers over the table's glossy, uneven surface; it was a soothing sensation, the shattered crags of enameled clay, whole in their fragments. I watched from my perch at the window, grateful for the buttery breeze airing out my fibres, which were pregnant with the smell of garlic and dill from that evening's dinner.

"Your father was crazy about your mother but so were most of the men in Tehran." Cala picked up a date from the box and popped it in her mouth. She strained her tea through the grainy sweetness. Minoo pulled her knees up into her body, wrapping her arms around her legs. The air was cool, but Minoo was grateful for the open window: the distant sound of neighbourhood kids playing a few doors down, Mrs Beswick opening her back door, the *thunk* of a garbage bag tossed into a can, the door closing a moment later. Bird chitter and occasional car passing. It reminded her of the wide, wonderous world outside herself.

That day, she'd left school after morning classes, run home, and called her mother. She'd had news—huge news: she'd just been cast in the lead role of their school play, *Alice in Wonderland*. She'd never auditioned for anything before. And she got the lead. She felt electric. Invincible.

She knew she shouldn't have called though. It was a Thursday, the beginning of the weekend in Iran and her mother had instructed her to not call on weekends because they were busy. But her body was buzzing with excitement, and it was so powerful, so overpowering; she felt like she'd implode if she didn't tell someone, and since Cala hadn't answered when she burst through the door, she called her mom. Because calling for our mothers is instinct as much as habit. It's hard-wired.

When her mother answered, Minoo blurted out the news. Her blood pumped into her brain so loudly that at first, she didn't notice her mother wasn't replying. She took deep breaths, trying to steady her heart and contain the smile threatening to split her face. But she still heard it: the unmistakable belly laughter of a child. Then, more laughter. Softer, deeper laughter, like a boulder bouncing down the side of a hill. She knew the register by heart: her father. Her father and her son. Their laughter grew louder, as if they'd just come into the kitchen where her mother was standing, as she always was when on the phone, by the small square table that held the phone, a notepad and pens.

What Minoo heard next was muffled. Her mother must have covered the phone receiver with her hand or buried it in her chest. Then, very clearly, with background laughter gone: "I told you not to call on weekends."

Minoo bit her lip and swallowed, then repeated her news, more slowly this time. Maybe she needed to impress upon her mother the weight of achievement. She got the lead. She was a new kid, and she was not only part of the theatre troupe but the star of the show. The director had said her audition had been mesmerizing. Had said she was the perfect Alice.

Her mother snorted. "Isn't Alice a flighty girl who doesn't listen to her mother and gets herself in trouble?" Minoo opened her mouth to respond, but her mother spoke first. "I've got to go. Be good and say hi to Ameh for me. And no more of this weekend calling." Minoo remained there with the receiver glued to her ear for a long moment. When she finally turned around, Cala and her friend Judith were standing in the kitchen entrance, paper bags of groceries in their arms. Minoo had no idea how long they'd been there, but judging by how still they were, assumed they must have been waiting to come in.

"Oh, azizam," Cala swept into the room, dropping her bag on the table and wrapping her arms around Minoo. Taking a step back, Cala pried the phone from her hand and hung it up.

"First off," Cala smiled, hooking her finger under Minoo's chin and nudging it up so her eyes came level with Cala's own. "Ghorboonet beram! I am so proud of you! This is amazing news!" She lifted the strap of her purse over her head and placed it on a kitchen chair. "Next," she clapped her hands together, "we're going to talk. We're going to talk about everything that just happened. But first, you go take a nice bath and Judy and I will make you dinner. Your favourite. Baghali Polo, right? We just got dill, and I think we have the fava beans too. Judy, would you check? I'm going to finish unloading the groceries. But this," she pointed to Minoo and herself then the phone, "this isn't over."

Having located a couple cans of fava beans, Judith headed out to help Cala unload the rest of the car, squeezing Minoo's hand as she walked by. Minoo felt like she was going to liquify, splash onto the kitchen floor. When Cala and Judith came back, there would be no sign of Minoo, only a puddle of goo. But then I caught Minoo's eye. My head was hanging out of the wicker mail basket on the hutch on the other side of the table. In those days, I had no permanent perch. And our relationship was new—Minoo didn't depend on me so much—so she was often leaving me laying around in strange, forgettable places. Being a sock, I was used to it. I didn't mind. She padded over and lifted me out, slipping me over her hand. I felt her fingers bend and flex in my skull, exploring the snug darkness of my mind.

"Really, Minoo," I said, affecting a wide, dramatic yawn and smacking my mouth. "I think we should take this as a win, as far as your mom is concerned." Minoo wrinkled her nose and tucked her chin back. "No, I mean it, my girl! Your mom basically admitted you were born for this role!"

Hugging me to her chest, Minoo chuckled.

"Your father loved your mother right away," Cala continued the story over tea and dates, "but I don't think affection came easily to her. Not that I have to tell you this. Your khâles were probably bedtime cautionary tales for you. But I knew them—all of your aunts, joonam—and as a young girl, I idolized them. They'd laugh and it was as if..." Cala closed her eyes, her head tilting to the side, like she was trying to locate their faces in her mind. She smiled. "It was as if their jaws would unhinge." Her eyes opened and she chuckled into her tea glass. "They allowed themselves to be fully alive."

Minoo rested her chin on her knee and remembered floating in the sea, starfished with the sunlight drenching her head to toe.

"I'd never seen anything like it."

Judith finished washing the dishes, wiping her hands on the back of her jeans. Stainless steel pots gleamed in the drying rack. Outside, Mrs Beswick's back door opened. Minoo heard the *pspspspsp* of her calling her old tabby Tom cat back inside for the evening, then the cat's throaty croak of greeting. Minoo could picture Mrs Beswick burying her face in the Tom's soft fur as she closed the door behind them with her foot.

"Your mother was always so serious. I think being born so many years after her older sisters left her too much in her own mother's orbit," Cala drew a circle in the air with her finger. "And your grandmother was bitter, so very bitter, after your grandfather left for who knows where or whom. No one talked of it, so I don't know the details. But I can't blame the girls for wanting to escape that bitterness. I was still a child then myself, but I remember my parents saying your grandmother held onto her daughters like a tick. Mesleh kaneh. She was going to lose them if she didn't unlatch. And mostly, she did."

It was completely dark outside. Judith emerged from the front hall, shrugging on her jacket.

"I can't say I know what became of them all," Cala tapped a fingernail on her tea glass, then pointed that finger at Minoo. "But I do know one, I think it was Shireen, became a dental surgeon and moved to Austria."

Coming up behind Cala's chair, Judith wrapped an arm around Cala's chest. Cala dropped her head back so she was looking up into Judith's face. Thank you, she mouthed. Judith planted a kiss on her forehead. Minoo looked away, down at her legs, at the Scottie dog print on her pajama pants. That affection; the rawness of it. It made her aware of every inch of her body. She rubbed her palms on her thighs.

Judith left and the front door clicked shut. Cala took her tea glass to the kitchen sink and stared out the window into the night.

"I'm sure it appealed to him," Cala said quietly. The clock on the kitchen wall ticked and tocked. She waved a hand and spun back to Minoo. "Your father, I mean. The seriousness. I think he saw stability in it. Your father's parents—you never met them—I suppose growing up with them could make a person crave stability." She took another sip of tea. "Do you know much of them?"

Minoo shook her head. All she'd ever been told was that they'd died before she was born. Car accident. Her father had just started his economics degree at university, and they'd left him with nothing, her mother said. "Absolutely nothing. Everything we have is because of our hard work. Nobody has ever helped us."

"They were lovely people in many ways—generous, kind. As a child, I didn't feel like family parties started until they'd arrived," Cala said. "And God, how they spoiled your father. An only child, like me. Only children in our family tend to be that way." Cala rested her hip against the counter and smiled, a dreamy slip of a smile. Minoo could almost see it: her remembering the children they'd been once. "Anything he asked for, they bought him," she snapped her fingers. "I remember they got him a dirt bike—an actual dirt bike. He was only seven and couldn't even ride a bike-bike, so of course, he hurt himself. Broke his arm. My parents had to take him to the hospital because his parents weren't there. Or, more accurately, they were there but weren't available. Addicts, you see. Opium. I think alcohol too." She waved her hand. "It doesn't matter. The point is they were passed out when he had the accident and he couldn't get them to wake up. We lived just down the street, thanks to God."

Cala paused. "You've really never heard this?"

Minoo shook her head again. Not a word.

"Tsk. I don't understand why people feel this need to marry their secrets, like they'll keep you warm at night. I've told your parents this. I told them that how they acted about you and the baby was ridiculous. I said…" Cala stopped, putting her tea glass on the counter. She took a deep breath. "What I said then doesn't matter now, joonam. My point is simply that if they'd told you more, it would have helped you understand them better. It could have helped you all."

Cala returned to the table and slid back into her chair, her face etched with weariness. Minoo pushed the box of dates closer to Cala. Cala smiled and picked one out of the box, taking a small nibble.

"Your father's parents… There were many wonderful things about them, but they were addicts and they were not good with money. People are people: never completely good, seldom completely bad. When your father's parents died, he was just a young man left with a lot of debt. He was close to losing his house—the house you grew up in—and having to drop out of school. My parents stepped in to help him, but it was a terrible time. And then he met your mother—through a school-friend's sister, I believe—and she was this bright, serious girl who was also very beautiful,"—Cala stopped to smile at Minoo—"just like you. And… I mean, I don't know for sure, everything happened so fast, and I was caught up in my own life and my schooling then, but I think having someone like her see him made him feel valuable. I only met her once before they were married. He brought her to meet my parents. My impression of her—and this may just have been due to the one psychology course I was taking at the time—but I thought she was so wildly unmovable and convinced of herself that she must also be very scared of something."

Cala reached for another date and rolled it between her fingers. "I'm not saying I know everything, but I do know, joonie, that none of it—none of what happened when you lived in Iran and none of what happened today—is your fault. Mifahmi?"

Minoo nodded, mostly because she knew Cala believed what she was saying, which felt good. To have someone convinced of the good in her.

"Your parents," Cala said, reaching a hand across the table to squeeze Minoo's arm. "You deserved better from them."

When Minoo left to live in Canada, her parents told everyone she was helping a relative recover from a difficult illness. Her parents told her that they'd follow her at a discrete interval with the baby. They told her this, but thinking back, she can't remember them promising her anything specific, because she had asked for specifics. Weeks? Months? She'd pleaded for assurances. She'd felt the icy release of fear flood her guts when she received none. And what is fear if not primal awareness of your own vulnerability.

"Enough!" her mother had shouted, startling the baby who'd been dozing in Minoo's arms. Her eyes were a freshly polished boot. "People are already talking, because of the way you fawn all over him." Minoo's mother seldom said his name back then. She must say it now. But at the time, her mother just called him baby or the baby or him. Minoo, on the other hand, said his name all the time. Davood.

Davood.

"They talk because of your," she flicked her fingers at Minoo's breasts, which her mother complained had grown substantially more noticeable, even under her manto. "We are uprooting our lives because of your mistake! Be grateful and stop with your questions!"

Standing at the airport, suitcase checked and boarding pass in hand, her body already ached for her baby. His syrupy scent. The perfect cup of his bottom in the palm of her hand. His velvety coos as she leaned over him and he tangled his plump fingers in her hair. But he was at home with her mother, to avoid a scene, her mother said. "You've already proven you have no self-control."

As she watched people walk through the security gates, a howl was building in her chest. It pushed against the bottom of her heart, her lungs. She asked her father, quietly, once more: When? He pressed his lips together, the whites of his eyes porcelain, about to break. He opened his mouth, then slammed it shut. Opened it once more and made a strangled whimper before spinning off into the crowd. And this, this clean, brutal break was the most honest answer she'd received and, all things considered, the most generous thing he could've given her.

Minoo and her parents were never together again after that day. The first time she heard her son speak was when she spoke to her mother the morning of the day before her wedding. Minoo and I were sitting on the bed in Cala's old room, now Minoo's room. Cala had moved out two weeks before and encouraged Minoo to move into the larger bedroom, to get used to life as lady of the house before Atanas moved in.

"Stake claim to it as your own, first," she'd said. Cala was staying with Judith. After the wedding, they'd officially move up north. "Make our escape!" Cala had winked, and Minoo was reminded of a movie she'd seen when she first moved to Canada. *Mary Poppins.* She'd felt the full body choke of despair when Mary left the children. She did not trust Mr and Mrs Banks—not one bit—to have really changed and become the parents Jane and Michael needed. Mary couldn't leave, she'd thought. She just couldn't.

Minoo picked at her worn comforter as she spoke with her mother. She was asking her, one more time, if she and her dad would come to visit after the wedding, since they'd said they couldn't come before. They'd given the usual reasons: a soccer game, a test that needed to be studied for, a commitment they'd made to help at the school. Whatever the reason, Minoo doesn't remember anymore because by then, she'd heard so many, and the subtext was clear: *don't blame us for not coming. We're taking care of what you couldn't.*

"I never asked to be a mother again in my forties," her mother often said.

"You never asked her to be, either." I always reminded Minoo.

The pause that resulted from her mother's exasperation at being asked again to visit when she didn't want to created enough silence for Minoo to hear a door slam closed, then the muffled sound of a low voice—her father. Then, silence again. She could picture her mother, shooing her father away. She wondered if her son had been with him.

Let's get one thing straight: Minoo didn't care if her parents were at the wedding, or if they met Atanas. She had a life here they'd never been a part of. More of her remembered life was here, without them. And she knew her father would be distant and reserved and her mother critical. The sofreh aghd wouldn't be right. *And why no sugar rubbing? No gol baroon? You care nothing for tradition.*

And her mother would be correct. Minoo didn't care about these traditions because she had learned that the word tradition, in her mother's mouth, actually meant convention, and that convention meant control. But she would have conceded to include all these things—the sugar sprinkled over the heads of her and Atanas to summon a life of sweetness, the sofreh with the two candles to signify light, the coins for wealth, a mirror for eternity, and eggs for fertility. And the gol baroon—the throwing of flower petals—and her mother's indifference and criticism. Minoo would have endured all of this if they'd just come, even if they hadn't brought the child, because if they were there, they couldn't just hang up or ignore her when they didn't feel like answering her questions.

Another peal of laughter and a call of greeting sounded in the background. Before she could stop herself, knowing that her mother usually answered questions about the boy with distance, disdain, or both, Minoo asked if that was him. *Davood.* She allowed herself to say his name out loud.

"He's a good, serious, child," her mother said by way of answering. "An excellent student." Minoo's mouth twitched, ready with a smart remark. Like most tyrants, Minoo's mother's pattern of cruelty was always predictable and easily provoked by slights to her ego. Asking how serious of a student the kid could possibly be at such a young age—he was merely eight years old—might have felt good in the moment, but it would have only lead to her mother denying Minoo what she wanted most: details. I clamped Minoo's lips shut with my own mouth.

"Ehm-em." I shook my head slightly. She narrowed her gaze but after a moment, sighed heavily through her nose. I held her eyes a moment longer before releasing my hold.

Instead Minoo asked if he was making any friends. Her mother snapped. "What does he need friends for? Stop pestering me with silly questions." And that was that. Her tap into her son's life had once again been turned off. She returned to the original question: Would they come for a visit after the wedding, at least?

"No," her mother had said, "that's not convenient either."

Minoo suggested she and Atanas could visit Iran instead, which was, Minoo realizes now, probably the worst thing she could have done.

"You." Her mother spat. "Always so selfish." The line went dead.

Minoo threw her body back onto the bed, covering her face with a pillow and screaming, screaming, screaming. When she was done and her throat burned from exhaustion,

I slid the pillow off her face and let it drop to the floor. Flushed cheeks, glistening eyes, heaving chest. That feeling, once again: total helplessness.

I pushed a sweaty strand of hair from her forehead. As far as I was concerned, it was just as well things were as they were. If her mother came, she would not have only criticized the wedding—the fact that it was so small and in Cala's backyard, which was what Minoo wanted. Her mother would have interpreted it as Atanas not being able to provide. She would have also reminded Minoo of how she wasted her time studying drama. Useless. And that Atana's economic degree was well and good, but what was he doing with it? Running a country bumpkin museum that paid so poorly they had to have a wedding in their home, which wasn't even really their home. Someone had given it to them, like charity. Disgraceful.

Ack.

And, I was quite certain, if Minoo had actually tried to fly to Iran, her mother would have moved house before the plane touched ground.

I fanned Minoo's face, trying to help her cool down. "You'd think if it was all downhill from here, gravity would at least have the decency to make it easier."

A COTTON BATTING EXISTENCE

At this rate, Minoo and I are never going to get home. First the police and now, we're stuck behind a farm tractor hauling a hay wagon loaded with round bales of straw. Black plumes of diesel billow from the exhaust pipe, the unmistakable smell filtering through the car's vents. The main street of town is as busy as it ever gets on a weekday. Boys on bikes shout to friends across the street. An older man in a jaunty bowling cap leaves the bakery with a white cake box. A guy Minoo went to high school with is having a cigarette outside the comic book store where he's worked since then. She can't remember his name but immediately recalls his smell: unwashed skin and scalp, so thick it would snake up her nostrils and coat the roof of her mouth. This boy, with his baggy cargo pants and anime T-shirts, sat beside her in one of their classes. World Issues, maybe. It was in the basement of the high school, and she can see his wide, full-moon face under fluorescent lighting. Him handing her a pen when she couldn't find hers. Laughing at some cheesy joke their teacher made when no one else would, his narrow shoulders shaking. He tosses the cigarette into an empty coffee can and disappears back into the store. He was kind, that boy. She remembers this.

Minoo glances at the time on the car's radio, not that we have anywhere we need to be. She, like me, is simply aware we should be home by now. It only takes ten minutes to get from the hospital to our house, a measure Minoo knows from the many times she drove Roya there for childhood fevers, earaches, and once, when Roya was twelve years old, for stitches. Roya got too close to the woodchipper Atanas had rented to clean up some storm debris and the machine spat out a splinter of wood, hitting Roya in the head.

Atanas had sped the familiar route to the hospital while Minoo sat in the backseat, pressing an increasingly blood-soaked towel to the deep gash in her daughter's eyebrow and praying that no debris had hit her eye. There was so much blood, she couldn't tell.

Minoo tries to recall if Roya cried when she got the stitches. How many stitches had there been? Minoo suspects her out-of-body panic has shattered the congruence of the memory. Certain specifics are lost. But she clearly recalls one moment, sitting on the exam table while Atanas waited for the discharge papers, with Roya calm and stitched and curled impossibly smaller than her twelve years into Minoo's lap like a sapling fiddlehead, like she hadn't done since she was very small—that still feels as immediate and clear as a cool marble in her hand. In that moment on the examining table with Roya sea-shelled in her lap and Atanas beside her, the world had shined. Her family was safe and whole, and for once, she wasn't questioning her completeness or the completeness of the love she was capable of giving to them.

But Roya was growing up; drifting away from childish roundness. She was all elbows. All knees. She was no longer interested in my stories. When her friends came over, she hid me, Pop Shoppe bottle and all, in the warming tray under the oven.

This growing distance was anticipated, of course, but expecting something rarely prepares you for the reality of its arrival. Time had unspooled; was unspooling around Minoo wildly. Ribbons of it were flying everywhere and she realized she'd never catch—never hold— it all. This seismic shift of certainty spoke to Minoo; she knew she'd waited long enough. Wasted too much time thinking her mother would come around. That night when they got home from the hospital, she called her mother and let her know that she and her family were coming to Tehran to see her son. She was not a child anymore. She was his mother. She had, she said, a right.

The line was silent. Minoo continued to stare at the ticking face of the kitchen cuckoo clock; a gift from Atanas, who'd seen how much Minoo had loved his Baba's when they'd visited her home in Plovdiv after they were first married. In less than a minute, an absurd little bluebird with a fur hat and bushy mustache would appear, chirp the hour, then retreat into its house.

Minoo heard her mother exhale. Then, her mother's cool voice: "Do you really think he even knows you exist?"

The bird popped out, chirped eight times, then slammed back into the dark body of the clock. Minoo dropped the phone to her side and turned to me. I'd been watching from my usual perch, the muted pink backdrop of evening outside the kitchen window. My head, improperly balanced on the bottle, tilted to the side; signalling an appropriate impression of concern.

We don't always know why people do what they do to us, and it's easy to let this uncertainty become part of who we are. Who we will become.

It hadn't occurred to Minoo that her son wouldn't know about her. Roya knew she had a brother. When she was old enough to do the math and realized just how young her mother had been, she had been less than impressed.

"Ew, Mom! Really?"

That evening Minoo started her second puppet: an elephant fashioned from a neon blue knee sock of Roya's. Its long, dangling nose was the foot of the sock. When, a few days later, Minoo asked Roya to name it, the girl recoiled.

"Mom," she put up a hand, "pass. Hard pass."

"I'll name it for you," Atanas came into the kitchen through the sliding door and put three meaty garden zucchinis on the counter. He wiped the dirt from his hands on his jeans.

Minoo shook her head. No, it was okay. She pecked his cheek with the puppet as if to say: *No hard feelings, though, right?*

To say, *It's no big deal.*

To say, *I love you but not in a way that will let me let you name this thing. This thing that came from me and me alone. That came from some shadowed, and barely recognized part of myself.*

To say, *If you name it, then it will always be part yours too, and you're already as much of my life as I can bear; tender as you are, as cloudlike in your love for me.*

Minoo didn't drink. Had never drank alcohol, in part because her mother would have disapproved and her disapproval cast a long shadow, and in part because Kit's father, whom Kit and her mom had left behind when they immigrated, was an alcoholic.

Kit had told Minoo of how her father's father was a drunk too, who'd beat her dad as a child. How her dad had bragged that at least he never beat Kit or her mom, as if that made the anger and hate and suspicion he directed at them better. He thought her mom was always cheating on him. That Kit didn't ask him for help with homework because she thought he was stupid for never having graduated high school. The truth was, Kit was a good student and didn't need help. And her mom wasn't cheating on him. Not at first, at least.

"The problem with alcohol isn't that it turns you into someone you're not," Kit said, twirling a toothpick of speared melon between her fingers. "It's that it turns you into who you are. Or," she popped the melon into her mouth and spoke from behind a hand, "one of the people." As Kit chewed, she scanned the party guests milling around them: all friends of Cala's and Judith's. The backyard was humming with them. They were there for Judith's retirement party from the labour union where she'd worked as a relation manager for thirty years.

"Early retirement party," Judith emphatically pointed out during her speech. "I know there's still work to be done, but quite frankly, I'm too tired to do it anymore. I look at the younger faces I see here tonight and know you'll carry the torch." Judith raised her glass and everyone cheered. She winked at Cala before taking a sip.

When the speeches were over, Minoo and Kit retreated to a table in the corner with plates of food. It was evening, but the sky still bled deep orange light at the edges. Paper lanterns hung from trees and pillar candles flickered on tables.

"We're not just one person, Minoo. Not even one type of person." Minoo watched as Kit dabbed at her lips with a napkin. The candle's glow flickered across her face. "None of us."

This, Minoo already knew. She knew that not all the people inside her were good, either, and she didn't want alcohol to let them loose.

The first night that Minoo met Atanas, she had agreed to join her classmates at the pub for the company, not the drinking. But that morning, as she was leaving her dorm room for her first class of the day, Minoo received an email from Cala.

SUBJECT: Picture
To: minoo.1982@hotmail.com
From: onlytahdig@hotmail.com

Minoo joon,

I've thought about whether or not I should send you this email, especially since we'll be seeing each other in a few days when you come home for a visit, but I think you've waited long enough.

Attached is a picture of your son.

He's in the front row, fourth from the left. The young man standing second from right at the back is my friend's son. He's the junior coach for the soccer team. His mother saw the picture and recognized your boy from seeing him around the neighbourhood with your parents, which put her in mind of me, and of course, you. Which is why she called. I mentioned you were away at university and doing well, which she was happy to hear and not the least bit surprised.

I also asked her if she could send me the picture.

My friend, like everyone else, thinks he's the child of your parents. I wanted to set the record straight, but I didn't because I know I won't be the one who suffers from ending this deception.

Do you still talk to your mother on occasion? My WhatsApp conversations with her, which as you know have never been exactly chatty, stopped altogether a while ago. (Did I tell you about that? When you were accepted for school last spring, she started asking for updates about you almost every day. I thought this would be a good time to remind her that you wouldn't be living with me soon, so if she wanted updates about you, contacting you—her daughter—directly, would be more efficient.)

I know my spot on her shit-list will definitely be secured after this email. But that doesn't matter.

You've wanted news of your boy for too long. Seeing this picture will likely be bittersweet, but I know you dokhtaram; it is not your nature to hide in darkness.

You don't need to open the attachment the moment you read this, but when you feel up to it, I think you'll be glad you did. You'll see what I mean. They can't really take him from you. You are undeniable.

Ghorboonet beram, xo

Cala

(Wait till you get home and we can open it together if you want!)

When Minoo looked away from her laptop, her eyes found mine where they were usually located those days: peering out from between stacks of books on her desk. My new perch. A place cluttered with water bottles and snack wrappers. Sometimes, I went along to rehearsals or drama classes—places where my presence was seen as an acceptable quirk, but most of the time, I slouched on my bottle, content, when Minoo was content. Worried, on days like that day, when Minoo was worried.

Drawing me off my bottle, Minoo pressed my curls into her face and inhaled before slipping me over her hand. The smell of home: lilacs and old wood. We faced each other. I nodded. Go ahead.

Minoo took a deep breath and opened the attachment. There he was.

My God, I thought. "Remind you of anyone?" Minoo sputter-laughed, bringing her fingers to her lips, opening her mouth as if to speak, then clamping it shut again. She began to cry. She touched his face on the screen. His dimples. His drawstring grin, hitched up in one corner. His hair, springing chaos and looking about ready to twirl off his head. Cala was right: Minoo was undeniable.

She left her dorm room electrified. Her first class was a blur. She fought the urge not to invite everyone back to her dorm to show them his picture, to proudly exclaim: *This is my son! Isn't he beautiful?* But she didn't. Not out of shame or fear of what people would think. She knew these people were not her mother. This was not the place of her birth. But she also felt that she wasn't ready to share him yet. She'd just seen him for the first time in six years. She needed to hold that magic without having to explain it.

She needed to hold it as long as she could.

As the day wore on, though, the charged feeling trickled to a stop and was replaced by a stony weight in her stomach. A feeling that could only be called—based on what she told me later that night, when she arrived home tipsy and thoughtful—longing. And longing, like the heat from a flame, has a way of distorting the world around you.

Minoo hadn't intended to drink that night.

Minoo hadn't intended to stay out as late as she did, either, which was why she found herself without a jacket on the walk home from the pub with her group of friends and acquaintances. The days were still warm, but the nights were cold enough to frost grass. She was cold, but less aware of it than she would have been sober—less aware of the languid droop of the moon, of the windows in the homes they passed, stuffed with warm, flaxen light. Buzzed and bubble-wrapped as she felt, she barely noticed these things. But Atanas, whom she'd just met as a friend of a friend of a friend of a friend, did. He noticed her wrap her arms around herself and squeeze. Their group had stopped at an intersection, waiting for the walk signal to change. Atanas pulled his sweater over his head, and when he did, the shirt he was wearing underneath hitched up, his stomach exposed. It looked impossibly hard and vulnerable; with a scant trail of fine hair leading under his belt. Seeing her staring, openmouthed, Atanas smiled, tugged down his shirt, then tossed his sweater at Minoo. It landed over her head, covering her eyes. By the time she'd pulled it off, Atanas was already crossing the street, a puff of vapor escaping his mouth as he laughed at whatever his friend was saying. The sweater retained his warmth. She'd hugged it to her chest and followed.

From the beginning, his tenderness has blunted the edges of her life.

The tractor comes to a halt in the middle of the street and Minoo, immersed in her thoughts, almost rear-ends the hay wagon. The operator—a man wearing a dingy-looking baseball cap, green coveralls, and rubber boots, hops out, waves at us, and jogs across the street toward a group of preteens on bicycles. One of the teens, a child in a floral summer dress, steps forward, embracing the man. He squeezes her briefly, before pulling his wallet out of a pocket and handing her a bill, which she excitedly waves above her head as she bounds into the gelato shop with her friends in tow.

He waves at us again before climbing back into the tractor and continuing forward. Minoo waits a few moments before following, looking into the shop as we pass. The kids have swarmed the counter. They're bouncing on the balls of their feet and pointing at the flavours in the glass display. The sudden rumble of Minoo's stomach startles us both. Her eyes jerk toward mine, shocked by the audacity of her body. Her stomach groans again, louder this time. I try to think back to the last time I saw Minoo eat. Not this morning, though Minoo hardly ever eats when she wakes up. Last night then? Yes. She'd warmed herself up some of the kashk-e bademjan Atanas had made a couple days ago, for Sunday lunch. After that meal, Atanas had fallen asleep on the couch, stretched out in buttery noonday light that dallied through the limbs of the maple tree outside the family room's picture window. He was understandably tired, having gotten up early that morning to start making the dish; one of Minoo's favorites, though not one she'd ever bothered to learn to make herself. Cooking never held any interest for Minoo, requiring her to put energy into something that disappears in moments. She's never seen the point. The meals she makes for herself are simple: bread and soft cheese. Salted cucumbers and pistachios. A scrambled egg with chunks of fresh dates. Atanas had asked Cala to teach him to make kashk-e bademjan. He'd come home with Minoo one weekend and saw how much she enjoyed the dish that Cala placed in front of her. Now it's Atanas who wakes in the morning—slipping out of the bed they still share, despite everything—to harvest ripe eggplants from the garden, caramelize onions, and crush garlic.

Despite everything because sometimes, love persists, whether you will it to or not.

The smell of garlic hung in the kitchen as Minoo poured herself a cup of tea. Bringing the tea glass to her lips, her gaze fell on the pans and plates Atanas had left sparkling in the drying rack.

She'd slipped me over her hand and together, we sought him out. In the family room, the radio was on low, the soft plunk of piano playing at the peripheries. Her eyes swept over his long form. The sleep of the dead, Minoo always said. Nothing could wake him: not a spaceship launch happening an inch from his face or, as was the case when Roya was a baby, his daughter wailing in the middle of the night. Even then, Minoo could never begrudge him his sleep. She'd climb back into bed, the indignant but subdued Roya suckling, and curl her body away from the dark heap of his sleeping form.

To be that untethered to the world… Minoo would drift off dreaming of that feeling.

Minoo placed her tea on the end table and crouched down beside the couch. Her fingers hovered over his lips: full and soft. She tried to remember the last time she'd kissed them, tried to muster some hunger for this man who she could recognize as beautiful: the aeolian ridges of his cheekbones and large, lithic hands. He was one of the most beautiful people she'd ever seen.

She pulled her fingers away and sat back on her heels, a familiar pneumatic feeling in her chest. Her nose twitched, like it always does when she's about to laugh. Her eyes welled with tears. A hand flew to cover her mouth, and she hiccupped, trying to swallow the sound that was strangled somewhere between a sob and guffaw. This confluence of emotion again; my poor girl.

"Minoo," I whispered. "It's okay." I tucked a spring of hair behind her ear.

"Hey," I said. "I have an idea." I opened the drawer of the end table. They were still there: dozens of tiny, coloured hair elastics, leftovers from when Roya was a child and would sit on the floor in front of Minoo to have her hair done. Braids, pony and pigtails—whatever Roya could dream of, Minoo would create while Roya ate her cereal before school and watched TV. The elastics: no one had bothered to remove them.

I dumped a mouthful of the little coloured bands onto the floor beside Minoo. She looked down then back up to me. My eyes blinked mischief. Hers blinked back, gleaming like creek-drowned pebbles. We both turned to Atanas. Drying her eyes on the back of my neck, a smile slinked across her lips.

Minoo has always been good with her hands.

While she worked, I was stretched out on the couch beside him, lacking the dexterity for such nimble labor. When he woke a little while later, Minoo and I were waiting, poised for his surprise, barely able to suppress the giggles. He sat up and patted his pincushion updo, eyes wide and mouth agog. Then, he'd laughed. He pulled Minoo onto the couch with him, into the warmth of his chest and she felt that safe, cotton batting existence.

"How do you put up with her nonsense?" I asked.

"Because," he said, not taking his eyes off Minoo's. "You make me smile."

The tractor turns left on a road leading out of town. Pale gold flecks of straw blow loose and dance in the air. Minoo follows them with her eyes. These moments never last, but it's nice to live among possibilities, just the same.

DELAM BERAT TANG SHODE

This is where things get muddled. Where lines blur.

Roya's baby hair was like peels of curled butter. She loved me then, without question. It's without question that I know she'd still love me if I'd had the grace to fade into the haze of all childhood things.

This is the problem, where lines get muddled.

We were sitting in the kitchen together: Roya, in her highchair. Me, trying to get her to eat breakfast. She had already refused yogurt, and we were on to blueberries, which she was also refusing, more intent on trying to suck my eye off my face; the round, gleaming green one.

Minoo wasn't being much help. She was on auto-pilot again. She'd had that dream she has every few months, where she's back in Tehran, and she's who she is now, as old as she is now. And she walks into her parents' home and there they are at table—and there he is, her baby. She allows herself to think of him like this in the dream, which makes it better. Which makes it worse. He's a little older than she ever knew him, but she still knows him. Her mother sees her and smiles and places her baby on the floor. He toddles up to her and she grabs him, lifts him onto her: the squish of his diaper in her hand, his hair under her nose; his fresh-squeezed baby scent. His supple flesh pressing between her fingers and the swell of her heart, about to burst. It's all so real, every time. And every time, Minoo wakes up encased in grief. Spends much of the day coated in the film of that dream. Delam berat tang shode. Your absence constricts my heart.

"Oh no no, joonam," I said, ducking out of range of Roya's mouth and pearly milk teeth again. "You could choke. Here." I passed her a blueberry. She took it from my mouth and mashed the berry into the tray of her highchair.

"You're supposed to eat those," I clucked. Roya continued to mash the blueberry with her palm and grinned, mimicking my clucking.

I plucked another berry from the bowl beside me on the kitchen table. The floor above us creaked and we both looked up.

"Dada." She lifted her chin to the ceiling and pointed a chubby finger skyward. The tender white of her creased neck often made Minoo sigh with pleasure. This was why she'd stayed home. She and Atanas had agreed she wouldn't go back to her job at the theatre, where she worked as stage manager, auditioning for plays when the part fit. Leaving felt like an easy decision back then. Minoo's commute was over an hour. Atanas's work was less than twenty minutes away and his job paid better than Minoo's. Another big reason: Cala had given Minoo a nearly fully-furnished house and Atanas's Baba had left him—her only grandchild—a modest inheritance. It made more sense for Minoo to stay home with Roya when she was little, and, if she wanted to, to stay home permanently. They could live comfortably off one income, Atanas assured her. She loved her work in theatre, but living in the distant reaches of the suburbs meant that even when Roya was school age it would cost the family almost as much in gas and before-and-after school care than it would bring home each month. Moving wasn't an option, either. Minoo loved her house. The first place she'd ever felt truly at home. So, she made what she felt was the most practical decision and slipped into the role of mom.

For a long time, it was enough.

And when it stopped being enough, because living as a fraction of yourself will always stop being enough eventually, she turned more often to me.

"Dada!" Roya squawked again.

"Yes, Dada." I dropped another blueberry in front of her. "It sounds like he's up. Why don't you finish your breakfast so you can play with him when he gets downstairs?"

Roya raised her hand in the air, happily drooling her dissent.

"Don't even think about it."

She brought her palm down on the berry. Splat.

"Goodness." I bit my bottom lip, surveying the berry guts and purple smears of carnage. "You're making quite the mess for your mama to clean up." Roya stopped mashing the berry and looked at me, eyebrows furrowed. Concerned.

"Oh my." I shook my head. "Whatever are we to do?"

"Oh my," Roya parroted.

"Maybe," I picked up the bowl and put it on her tray. "Maybe, if your mama has to clean up anyway, we should at least—" I nosed the berries toward her. "We should at least make sure that it's worth it."

Roya looked down at the bowl, then to me. I wiggled my eyebrows. She giggled. I wiggled again. Then, looking only briefly at Minoo, who was looking at us without seeing a thing, she lifted the bowl as far above her head as her small arms would allow and let the berries fall.

This is the problem. Roya thought I was there for her, but she misunderstood: she wasn't who I was made for.

THE MORE I WANT OF THE SKY

A few months ago, Minoo had a doctor's appointment for some pain she'd been having in and around her chuchul. That's what she still calls it. I swear, if my eyes weren't sewn to my face, I would have rolled them. I remember swearing inwardly, wondering why she continues to use these childish terms. She's been an adult for longer than she was a child, and she knows the proper word in Farsi. She knows the proper word in English: vagina. It's a word that's lovely to say in English, even, mythologic in vibration and free as it is from the cold anatomical edge of so many other body parts. Spleen. Penis. Anus.

But chuchul.

Even box would have been better. Cooch, I could stand. Pelvic region, for god's sake, because if we wanted to be precise, month after month, the pain bloomed through the entire area: from hip to hip and lower. But on the phone, she'd actually said chuchul to the doctor's receptionist, who either knew (or what's more likely—inferred) what Minoo meant by her lowered voice.

The day of the appointment, Minoo begged me to come with her, but I managed to remain at home, reminding Minoo that many doctors already have trouble taking their female patients seriously.

I am not altogether foolish, you see. Impatient and sometimes judgmental, yes. But not a total dolt.

That morning, Minoo and I sat on the front steps wrapped in a floral quilt. It was Minoo's favourite blanket, made by Atanas's grandmother decades ago. It seemed on the verge of disintegration and, for years, Minoo had been reluctant to use it, frayed and faded as it was, but Atanas had insisted.

"Don't we all deserve to be held, especially as we fall apart?" he teased. And if I hadn't come to understand Atanas already, I would have understood him perfectly then. Atanas, with the dawdling green eyes and unbothered set of his mouth. Who couldn't be pushed to raise his voice or criticize, even when we deserved it. Atanas with the perpetually wind-swept looking hair, the perfect length to tease around a finger. It's easy to see how someone could fall in love with him. Minoo has never wondered, not for one moment, why she did. What she sometimes wonders is, if it was enough. If it is the kind of love you are supposed to feel for the person you marry.

Sometimes, she still questions this.

As she's gotten older, she's become less easily seduced by popular narratives of love and desire. Most days, she can accept that the kind or quantity of love she thinks she is supposed to feel is irrelevant. She lives with the kind of love she is capable of giving.

And most days—so many days—she's grateful for the companionable grace that has settled between her and Atanas, and for the existence of a woman named Dorcas, who inhabits a space Minoo used to force herself to fill. Dorcas, who is known in town for having married young and survived the twenty years she was trapped with her now incarcerated and now ex-husband. Dorcas, who three years ago, sold the large house her family had lived in together and moved into a little apartment above the local cannabis dispensary, and who now spends two months of the year with her son's family in Italy, two months with her other son in Halifax, and two months traveling by herself—absolutely by herself—wherever she pleases.

Minoo is grateful for Dorcas because she shows Minoo there are more ways to be alive and be in love than she'd ever allowed herself to imagine.

And what a gift, right? What a beautiful, excruciating vision to be gifted, when you are stuck.

Last week, when we'd popped into town for some bone meal for the roses, we drove past Atanas and Dorcas sitting outside the cafe on main street. He was laughing at something she'd said, his rambunctious curls shaking and mouth open to inhale the fool blue sky. Dorcas's face was radiant, her hands were clasped at her lips, as if holding in pure bliss.

It wasn't the first time we'd seen them together. Everyone in town had been seeing Atanas and Dorcas together for years, and while the couple were never openly affectionate in public, no more than two friends might be, you could tell by the way Atanas smiled to himself when Dorcas talked expressively, waving her arms around, or the way Dorcas watched his mouth as he spoke, that there was more. For a few months the speculation and scandal circulated, with all the usual gossiping and side-eyeing. However, as no one involved wanted to talk about it—not Atanas nor Dorcas nor Minoo could be moved to confirm or deny—the town lost interest and quietly accepted the arrangement.

Roya must know about it too. I had pointed this out to Minoo one evening, probably about six or seven years ago now, when Roya was at a friend's house and Atanas was, presumably, out with Dorcas. Gossip seemed to be dying down about the whole affair, as far as Minoo could tell. People didn't hush when she walked into a store. She didn't look up from reading a food packaging label to find someone's eyes on her. Well-meaning Mrs B had stopped asking her over for tea every time she didn't see Atanas's car in the driveway at night when he'd usually be home. Things seemed to have fizzled and that night, we were stretched out on the couch watching *Harvey*, one of Minoo's favourite movies. And mine too, for obvious reasons. The main character, Elwood P. Dowd—an unassuming and good-natured drunk—is presumed crazy for his belief in his friend, Harvey, a clever and mischievous six-foot white rabbit no one else seems to be able to see or hear. Elwood's family tries to have him committed but a series of hilarious and fortuitous snafus occur that leave one to wonder who's really bananas.

Minoo continued to munch on popcorn, brushing off my concerns like kernels from her T-shirt.

"Yes, she's just a child but that doesn't mean she's blind," I argued.

I reminded Minoo of her own childhood, and how she may not have understood a great many things, but she understood far more than adults gave her credit for. She'd understood that her father loved her, but loved her mom more. She'd understood that her mother was high-strung, almost always. She may not have grasped the hows or whys—and she definitely didn't understand that her mother's constant anger stemmed from being afraid to lose control until she was much older—but she had seen things.

"Roya sees too." Minoo stopped munching. "Do you think other parents don't talk in front of their kids and those kids don't talk to Roya? They're teenagers for god's sake."

Minoo paused the movie and sat up, popcorn kernels falling from her chest to the ground. On the screen, Elwood was frozen with his back to us, placing a painting he'd commissioned of Harvey and himself on the mantel. In the picture, Elwood sat wearing a suit and tie and an easy grin. The rabbit wore a jaunty bow tie and was positioned beside him, an arm draped comfortably over Elwood's shoulders. Minoo wondered about getting a little bow tie for me. She could make one easily enough. Cut up an old shirt or something. And I wouldn't wear it everyday, only when we went out somewhere nice. When I needed to look a little more distinguished. Minoo's eyes were measuring my face, thinking through her totes and drawers of craft supplies. I needed to stop this. We were drifting. "Minoo," I snapped. "Let's focus. Roya."

Minoo flopped back down. She popped another kernel of popcorn in her mouth and chewed without enthusiasm.

"Need I remind you, that while Roya is still a child, she is also a teenager—and teenagers, even with perfectly normal and well-adjusted parents are mortified by their parents' very existence and this—whatever the hell this is—is not normal or well-adjusted. So, if she knows about her father and Dorcas, which she almost certainly does, it's not exactly like she's going to tell you about it."

Minoo was silent. She stopped chewing.

"So you might want to talk to her. Talk to Atanas about it and then talk to her, together. Form a united, supportive front, you know?" Minoo nodded, a fleck of popcorn stuck to her lip. "You used to watch *Dr Phil.* I bet that's what he would tell you." I snuggled back into the couch with her, feeling satisfied with our little talk. "Now press play."

It's no surprise that Minoo never spoke with either of them. But as Harvey would tell you, there's only so much we fabricated friends can do. People are going to fix or mess up their lives, with or without us. Minoo continued to go about her day-to-day, not uninformed, exactly, but refusing to be too aware. To be too afraid.

Seeing Dorcas and Atanas last week felt different though: a wall, cracked. When we pulled into the greenhouse parking lot, Minoo sat for a moment, puffed up, holding her breath before her body collapsed forward, forehead slamming into the steering wheel, which I was still clutching. She lifted her head a few minutes later, eyes glistening and irises lightened from their deep chestnut to their post-cry hen's egg brown. Her lips were pillowy and darkened by the rush of blood to her face. Minoo was always pretty when she cried, but especially more recently. A good tear-induced swell contrasts the age-related loss of fat in her cheeks.

"You can still have that, Minoo." I pushed her hair off her forehead and offered her a rumpled takeout napkin that had been shoved in the cup holder. It was stained brown with tea, but it was a better option than her resorting to using me as a snot rag. Which she's been known to do.

"You can still have what they have." Minoo shook her head, but straightened herself in her seat and cleared her throat. She blotted the napkin under her eyes. The intimacy of that scene had been agonizing, I knew. Agonizing in the way certain moments reminded us that life isn't over, we've simply chosen to not be a part of it. In the way it reminded us that we're the reason we don't have what we want.

Atanas and Dorcas, shimmering there in the sun, light crashing off their water glasses, had reminded her of Kit. The unbearable memory of the heat of Kit's fingers laced through her own. How her thoughts would pop like soap bubbles whenever Kit was near.

Minoo doesn't talk about Kit anymore and she thinks that means she's over it. Whatever it was. Minoo is not being dismissive when she thinks this. Not entirely. She really doesn't know what it was, and when you can't define something, it's easier to pretend it isn't real. But of course, Kit was real. She is real and with Minoo everyday. Kit named me, after all.

Minoo gathered her purse and wiped at her nose with the napkin. She straightened her back, preparing herself to go into the nursery, to buy the bone meal and smile at any neighbours she may encounter. Minoo shoved the sodden, disintegrating napkin into the map pocket of her door and pasted on a smile.

"Looks mangled as a wad of bubble gum." I said. She huffed, ripping me off her hand and tossing me onto the passenger seat then slamming the door.

Understand, Minoo was not born to performance, but she was born to loneliness, and that's a precursor. The morning of her doctor's appointment, while Minoo was trying to sway me from my decision not to accompany her to the clinic, I watched the light burn mist off our still quiet street. We'd lived on this street for twenty-seven years, with its Victorian red brick houses with gingerbread trim and original wood floors that were, in the case of our home, warped in places and blanketed with thick Persian rugs. The same rugs that had been here when Minoo lived in the house with Cala. Cala had come into a small fortune when her father died, a few months after her mother's passing—a broken heart, Cala said. He'd left Cala, his only child, complete ownership of his thriving textile plants. She promptly sold the business and moved to Canada. Canada, because it was far away from Iran and the memory of her parents and the limitations it placed on women. And Canada because it was not the USA. And Ontario because that's where Toronto was, and Toronto was the only city in Canada she'd heard enough about to be able to picture in her mind. "You don't have to know exactly where you are going, aziz," she'd told Minoo, "but you do have to have an idea." Once she'd lived in Toronto for a couple years, she decided she loved the culture but not the crowds, so she moved a little out of the city to a quiet town that was still close enough to the highway to get downtown in about an hour.

A week before Minoo married Atanas, Cala informed her that she was moving to an even smaller township in central Ontario with her friend, Judith. They'd bought a small house on Lake Nipissing where they could drink tea and watch the sun rise and set every day.

"The older I get, the more I want of the sky," Cala said. "I want the sky in water and the sky above me too. Both of us do." Her smile as she spoke had the vague, lingering quality of a dream. "And now, you have given us the perfect excuse to do so." Cala's expression cleared and she gripped Minoo by the chin, squeezing her mouth into a pucker. "Ghorboonet beram! I thank God everyday for you, you know that, right?"

The house, Cala went on to explain, would be left as a gift to Minoo.

Initially, Minoo had been more anxious than grateful. What would she do without Cala? That soft spot in her life. It hadn't taken Minoo long after arriving in Canada to love Cala completely. Cala and her perpetually bubbling samovar, overflowing bowls of fruits and nuts, and the bright and babbling stream of women always coming and going through the doors of the house. Women in leather pants and cargo shorts and jeans embroidered with birds of paradise and lilies on their back pockets. Women with tattoos and scars and piercings and purple hair and long hair and spiky hair and undercuts; who'd smelled of cigarettes and pipe smoke and perfumes and colognes; who'd hugged Minoo longer and more gently than she'd ever been hugged in her life.

"You are ready for this," Cala said, taking Minoo's hands in hers and shaking them so the silver bangles on Cala's wrists jingled. "But you must understand: this house is yours and only yours. Atanas, he's a nice boy, but every woman needs something a man can't touch." She explained this firmly but not unkindly while they sat exactly where we sat the morning of Minoo's appointment. On the porch steps, their faces lifted to the sun.

I tried to remain as firm as my fibres would allow while Minoo pleaded with me to accompany her to her doctor's office. She said that I had to go, that her words wouldn't come out right if I wasn't there. I watched the spiny silhouettes of pine trees give in to colour; the day's demand for clarity.

"No, Minoo." I took the quilt in my mouth and tugged it snuggly across her shoulders. It was May, and the mornings weren't really that cool. My gesture was meant to comfort. "Just think about it," I said. "Imagine yourself trying to talk to the doctor with me there? Trying to explain how it feels as if someone has reached into your body and grabbed your womb, twisting and squeezing it to pulp? And about the maniacal bloating and exhaustion? And the pressure? That, no, it's not your period. It's constant. And no, it doesn't go away with painkillers. And yes, you have tried warm baths, and nothing works. And all the while you're saying this, I'm there—picture it, really picture it"—I paused, picturing it. Giggles bubbled in my throat. As if catching them in her own, Minoo emitted a squeak—"And all the while I'm there: nodding along like some piled, woozy-eyed jack-in-the-box?"

Minoo and I tried our best to consider each other seriously, eye to eye, to really absorb the seriousness of the situation, for this was serious business; but Minoo squeaked again, and that's all it took. We began to shriek with laughter.

"I bet that would get the doctor to finally do something… like send you to the psych ward!" I dabbed at Minoo's ecstatically watering eyes with the tip of my nose.

"What else is there to do but laugh, my Minoo?"

Our frailty being inevitable as it is.

Minoo's diagnosis would take months. And wouldn't really be a diagnosis as much as a best guess because the tests—the ultrasound, MRI, CAT scan—came back clear.

Ovulation. The doctor said ovulation was causing the pain. That, and the stage two pelvic prolapse, but we already knew about that. Had known since her mother had taken her to their family doctor in Tehran for a post-baby checkup. The doctor, her mother said, could be trusted. Would be discreet. After the examination, he'd clucked his tongue.

"Pregnancy in one so young is hard on the body. Just because your body supported a child doesn't mean it was ready to."

He'd given Minoo exercises to do, which she forgot about. Being as young as she was, she didn't understand the ways her body could fail her. She was the sort of person who preferred to think of her insides as white marble: polished and unchanging. But the prolapse became worse after Roya, which is why Roya was their only child. This is the reason Minoo gave Atanas for not wanting more children, at any rate. When Minoo thinks about it—on those rare occasions she allows herself to—this was only partly true. True, because she didn't like to think of the mess inside her body: raw and red and sagging and damaged beyond repair. Loose and floppy.

A loose girl.

But also, not true, because after Roya was born, the doctor had said there were corrective measures. She could repair her pelvic floor and have another baby. But Minoo had waved the doctor off. She had her child, and she got to keep her. Atanas, to his credit, did not push it. Occasionally, she'd even allow herself to melt into him when he reached for her at night, but after a time, that stopped too, draining slow like snow melt from the eves, until one day, it had been months, then years, since they'd touched each other that way.

By the time she got home from the final appointment where the doctor explained the probable diagnosis, it was early afternoon. Late summer. The day had grown soupy with heat. I helped Minoo gather her hair into a ponytail and then poured her a tall glass of iced tea. Then another. Then another and another. Then we settled into the couch with a fifth sweating glass. She drained half of it right away.

"You're going to piss yourself."

She burped discreetly behind her fist.

"Very couth. Your mother would be so proud."

Just then she admitted to me that she didn't really know what ovulation was. Had been too embarrassed to ask the doctor. She'd looked it up on her phone when she got back into the privacy of her car. Then she looked up pelvic prolapse. Which prompted her to have to look up cervixes. She hadn't known what a cervix was. Had no idea she had one. But she closed the search when she grew afraid the result might show a picture. She said all this without looking at me, staring intently at the ice in her drink.

"How does a grown woman not know what ovulation is? What a cervix is?" I asked. "How does a grown woman freak out at the prospect of seeing a picture of a cervix—a body part she has?"

Minoo shrugged, sipping her tea through a corkscrew straw. I sighed. "Where's your phone?"

Minoo looked around, patted her pockets. "Or the laptop. Or tablet. Get me something I can search with."

After we settled back down with the tablet, I began my search.

"Activate the microphone," I ordered. Minoo tapped the microphone symbol.

I made sure to speak clearly. "Cervix picture."

Minoo whipped her face around to me, terrified. Wide-eyed.

"No," I said, refusing to meet her gaze but feeling it boring into the side of my head. "You're not getting out of this. Don't even try. You say 'cervix' and scrunch up your nose. You look mortified when I want to show you what one looks like. Minoo, it's what you look like. You understand you have one in you—in your body, right now, right?" I nodded toward her crotch, then tapped the first, small image to get a better look. "You get that Roya has one, and Cala, and all the women you love. Even your mother has a cervix."

Minoo sucked her lips into her mouth. I continued.

"I think it's time you learn what you look like, inside out. Then maybe you can stop being so ridiculously skittish all the time."

Images loaded onto the screen: pink mounds with black holes. Some holes were small, the size of the head of a corsage pin. Some were larger, and not really holes at all but slits. Some with blood or mucus dribbling out. I admit I was not any more prepared for these images than Minoo. It was an effort to keep my voice smooth. Light. Controlled. Because that was sort of the point, right? To force Minoo to confront the dark places in herself.

The screen of cervixes was perhaps drastic, but Minoo's ignorance annoyed me, and I wanted her to shock her out of her apathy. I wanted to shame her out of her fear of herself and her body and what it needed. What it had always needed.

I recognized, though, that my strategy was flawed. Minoo was already ashamed. My existence was proof enough of this.

I was here because Minoo was too scared to be. And anyway, I knew the answer to my question: Minoo didn't know about her cervix or prolapse or ovulation because her body was, and had always been, a wound she'd had to endure.

As I scrolled through the cervixes and felt Minoo's tension in every bone in my body, I tried to soften my approach; reframe it not as a punishment, but an adventure. I stopped at a picture. *Twenty-five-year-old female, no children*, the caption read. A thick strand of pearly goo drooled from a little black opening. I nodded toward it.

"Look at this one! Looks like it's fallen asleep with its mouth open!"

A strangled squeak erupted somewhere inside Minoo's chest. I scrolled a little further.

"And that one!" I swung around to find Minoo squinty-eyed. "Minoo, look!" I tapped the screen. *Thirty-eight-year-old female, third child, six weeks postpartum*. "This one looks like it's smiling at you!"

She snorted.

"I mean, how can you be afraid of something that clearly likes you so much?" All it took was this question, delivered with deadpan seriousness, and Minoo exploded into raucous convulsions. She flung me to the couch then beelined to the bathroom, holding herself between the legs like a child, bursting and incontinent with laughter.

That day, I felt, we may have made some progress.

But progress is rarely linear.

BRUISED LIPS AND OPEN HEARTS

From our bedroom, Minoo and I watched Kit dawdle up the stone walkway leading to the front porch. She waved over her head to her mother, who was honking goodbye as she drove away.

"I bet her armpits smell like ice cream," I whispered. Minoo giggled, burying a dimple in her shoulder.

Kit stopped to talk to Cala, and Cala, kneeling in the flower bed pulling weeds, said something that made Kit throw back her head and laugh. The flash of her throat, its long pale column, sent Minoo scurrying from the window onto the bed. There we sat, Minoo's body electric, static frisson coursing through my fibres. We heard the front door open, then softly close. The sound of Kit's quick, light flight up the stairs. Kit bursting into the room, one hand on the doorknob and the other extended overhead. The smile exploding from her face.

"Tonight's the night, baby!"

Kit flung herself across the room and onto the bed, pulling us down beside her then promptly flipping herself over onto her hands and knees above our body.

"Are you ready to MOSH!?" Kit bounced so we flopped around wildly, laughing helplessly. Kit stopped and sat back on her heels. She brought my face to hers. "Whaddya think EP?" The spray of freckles over her cheeks crinkled. "Do you think she's up to it?"

I turned to look down at Minoo. We'd spent an hour trying to tame her hair with a flatiron, but wisps were already beginning to frizz out again. Irrepressible, I'd called it. *Unmanageable,* her mom would have said. The heat from the insides of Kit's thighs was making Minoo flush. From the base of her neck to the tips of her ears bloomed red. And Minoo, apple-cheeked and hammer-hearted, was grinning beneath us. I turned back to Kit, who couldn't have been oblivious to this. Always, I've maintained that Kit knew—she knew exactly how Minoo felt. She knew because she felt it too. If she hadn't, she wouldn't have touched Minoo as often as she did: picking fuzz out of her hair; hooking her pinky around Minoo's when they walked, arms swinging; pulling her close and lowering her voice to say the simplest of things.

We should see that movie tonight.

Where did you say Cala buys these dates again?

Sing that song about the cow again.

Hasan's cow. The song she'd sung to her son and her mother had sung to her. Minoo sang it to Kit, softly at first, then louder as the rhythm of the song rooted itself. Atal matal tootoole! Govee Hasan che joore? By the end of the song, Minoo would always grab Kit by the wrists and clap her hands together in time. They'd laugh, and Minoo would think of how she'd taken her son's wrists in her hands just the same way—those wrists, with their delectable folds of baby fat—and how they'd laughed together too.

Minoo never told Kit about her son, but in her head—in her dreams of the future where there was her and Kit, there was also, always, her child. One of his small hands in each of theirs. Because Kit wouldn't have cared. Minoo can still picture the slight part of Kit's lips when Kit leaned into her in the bathroom at the immigration centre. Minutes before, they had been lounging in the common room after English lessons. Watery light poured through the floor-to-ceiling windows and bathed Kit's skin in a mother-of-pearl sheen.

Kit had caught Minoo staring. "What's the matter?" Kit patted her cheeks, forehead, and nose. "Do I have something on my face?"

Minoo shook her head, fumbling for a reason she'd been ogling her friend. She ended up asking how she'd managed to get her eyeliner so thin. Which it was—precise as calligraphy—but Minoo had never actually wondered about it. It was part of the magic of Kit, and Minoo wasn't interested in lifting the veil.

But when asked about it, Kit beamed, delighted. She jumped out of her chair.

"A steady hand, kjæreste!" Kit grabbed her backpack, then Minoo's hand and dragged her to the bathroom. There, she schlepped her pack onto the counter and brought out a small, floral-print makeup bag. "Move closer, I'll show you." Without waiting, Kit grabbed Minoo by the waistband of her jeans and tugged her in. There was less than a pin's length between them, hip to hip.

As Kit began to work, Minoo felt the cool black liner settle between her lashes.

"My dad used to hate it when my mom put on makeup." Kit's breath was warm with the nostril-tingling spice of her cinnamon gum. "Took it as proof of her infidelity.

Which was total bullshit because when she didn't put on makeup, he said she didn't care enough about looking good for him."

She stepped away, tilting her head to the side to assess her work while chewing thoughtfully. "Really, I feel sorry for the guy." She stepped in again. "Hold still." She blew on Minoo's lashes, then popped the applicator wand out of the tube again. "Can you imagine going through life being so insecure and sad that you have to try to control the most inconsequential things about the people around you?" She shoved the applicator back into the bottle and screwed on the lid. "There, perfect!" Kit dropped the eyeliner back into her bag and zipped it up. She spun Minoo toward the mirror. "Look!"

Minoo blinked. The eyeliner was almost imperceptible, but had the effect of making her eyes, dark as the mouths of baby birds, seem even hungrier. Kit laced her arms through Minoo's and around her waist. She rested her chin on her shoulder.

"But of course, you were perfect before," she pecked Minoo's cheek. "Don't let anyone tell you different."

So Minoo felt, with unarticulated certainty, that Kit would have understood it all. She would have understood about Minoo's son. Would have understood about having to leave Iran and come here. She would know about being a disappointment to someone, maybe not because you are who you are, but because they are who they are. Kit would get how someone could become the horrible thing they're accused of being, simply by being accused of it long and hard enough. The thing was—the reason Minoo hadn't told Kit about any of it yet—was because at that point, Minoo didn't completely understand herself..

Not yet.

But Minoo thought she would tell Kit everything. Eventually. Sharing with Kit the song she sang for her son was a first, tentative step toward that shared life.

Kit had come over to Minoo's that afternoon—had bounded into her room like a happy puppy— because they were going to a concert that night. Some indie band that Minoo had never heard of but Kit loved. In the preceding weeks, Kit had explained the concept of the mosh pit. Not that Kit knew firsthand—she'd never been in one—but some school friends had told her about what to expect. Bodies slamming into each other. Bruises. Bumps. Frenetic energy.

"Sounds awesome, right?" Kit had said. Minoo wondered about the sort of friends Kit hung out with at her school—kids unconcerned by the dimensions and implications and complications of their bodies. So unconcerned that they'd willingly smash them into other bodies.

"I know one guy who couldn't turn his head left for weeks after his first one!"

Minoo hoped the widening of her eyes would be interpreted as excitement.

Kit also told her to wear something comfortable. Not too many layers. "Gets hot in there." Kit winked.

Kit was wearing loose army-green cargo pants that settled low on her hips and a grey tank top cropped just above her belly button; enough to show her soft stomach. Soft as in her skin, yes. But also, soft as in not hard. Soft as in the little pillow of fat cradled between her hips. Soft as in soft enough to make Minoo want to bury face in that flesh and inhale her whole.

Before Kit arrived, Minoo had lined her eyes just as Kit had taught her; a contrast to Kit's eye makeup for the evening, which was severe. Smudged black liner, steely shadow.

"You're not dressed!" Kit, who was still hovering above us, snapped the waistband of Minoo's sweatpants then turned to me. "She's not dressed! Why isn't she dressed?!" Kit hopped off the bed and pulled Minoo to her feet.

She hadn't been able to decide what to wear. I hadn't been much help. After the ordeal of straightening her hair, we only managed to rifle through her closet for a couple minutes before we gave up entirely. Minoo had never been to any concert, let alone the type that Kit described, and she was at a loss as to what to do. What to wear. How to stand. She'd practised in front of the mirror on the back of her door. Her mouth set in a hard line, her eyelids lowered, mysterious.

I shook my head. "You look drugged."

She opened her eyes wide, smiled huge.

"Now you look another kind of drugged."

Minoo pulled the chair out from her vanity and flopped down. Earlier that afternoon, Cala had given her a pair of fishnet stockings to wear, though with what, Minoo couldn't imagine. I helped Minoo slip her other hand into a stocking leg and down to the foot, marveling at the criss-cross pattern. I watched an idea spark to life. She was thinking of what this stocking could become: a saucy, pouty-lipped seductress with long, purple yarn hair and ostrich feather eyelashes. Lips fashioned from the red cheese wax. But her thoughts had been cut short by the sound of a car slowing in front of the house. Minoo threw the stockings over the dressing table mirror to see if it was Kit.

And it had been.

"These," Kit said, plucking the stockings off the mirror, "are perfect!"

Kit yanked open her dresser drawer and rummaged through its contents until she found a pair of light blue ripped jeans. “Perfect.” Kit grinned, then in one, fierce rip, made the rip bigger, extending it from knee to hip. She tossed the stockings and jeans on the bed and disappeared into the closet.

“You have a lot of space in here and not nearly enough clothes to fill it.” Kit’s voice was muffled. “Such wasted potential.” When she emerged, she held a top in each hand and had a couple more thrown over a shoulder.

“Come here.” We met her in the middle of the room on a little round braided area rug. She held each top up to Minoo’s chest, shaking her head and hurling them aside until she landed on a black vest.

“Yes!”

Minoo looked panicked. The vest had a deep V-neck and was meant to be worn as part of a suit. With a blouse. Minoo pointed this out: that there was a shirt to go under it.

“No there isn’t,” Kit flicked a glance at Minoo before beginning to collect the discarded shirts from the floor. A moment later, from inside the closet, her voice boomed: “Stop standing there and get dressed!”

In the backseat of Judith’s car on the way to the venue downtown, while Cala and Judith chatted in the front and Kit talked excitedly beside her, Minoo could only think of wind from the open window rushing over her bare shoulders. Under the neckline of her vest.

Finally fully dressed and standing in front of her bedroom mirror an hour earlier, Minoo had been stunned at the person she saw, who was not so much unrecognizable, as unbelievable. She liked it and was ashamed to like it: the cinch of her waist, the curve of her hips and breasts, all clearly visible. Minoo and I had continued to fuss with her hair, but Kit gently drew her arms down to her sides.

"I'd kill for your lips." Kit turned Minoo toward her and patted a rusty stain into place with a finger. Their eyes met in the mirror. A thrill of electricity flashed up Minoo's spine.

As they approached the venue—a dingy looking building on the corner of otherwise immaculate storefronts, Cala turned in her seat to remind the girls of the pick-up details: She and Judith would be hanging out with some friends who lived nearby. At 11 p.m., when the concert was over, they'd come get them. Cala pressed a piece of paper into Minoo's hand.

"Here's the number at the apartment if you need anything," she said. "Anything. We can be here in five minutes."

She squeezed Minoo's hand. Judith smiled at her in the rearview mirror. Minoo tucked the paper into a jean pocket and stepped out of the car, shutting the door behind her. Kit was already bounding to the lineup, which was on the verge of snaking around the street corner. They were early. Kit had said that if girls wanted to get a spot in the mosh pit, it was easier to start there than have to fight to the front.

"Come on," Kit shouted over her shoulder, waving.

Minoo turned back to Cala.

"You look incredible." The skin around Cala's eyes crinkled. Fanned like a mermaid tail. "But maybe leave that with me?"

Minoo looked down. I was looking back up at her, dumbly. She relinquished me through the window.

"We'll see you later," Cala said, placing me against her chest and patting my head.

"Minoo!" Kit shouted. "COME! ON!"

Later that night, finally in bed, Minoo pulled the blanket over our heads and rolled onto her side. We were face to face in darkness. Her pepperminted breath was slow, deliberate. I could feel the hammer of her heart in my neck.

"Whenever you're ready," I whispered. Cala slept at the other end of the hall, with a bathroom and a linen closet between them, so I didn't need to whisper for her sake. I whispered for Minoo, who I was afraid would bolt like a jumpy goat if I spoke too loud, moved too fast. I waited.

"Minoo..." I wasn't the best at waiting.

Ever since we'd picked them up after the concert, Minoo had been spring-loaded. It was nothing you could see, on the outside—Minoo had learned to restrain her emotions when necessary. But I could feel the tension as soon as I settled over her hand: the skittishness. A flicking, nervous energy.

"How was it?" Cala twisted around in her seat and smiled at the girls. Kit and Minoo, who'd been buckling their seat belts, looked at each other, then at Cala in unison.

Minoo answered first, quickly, her dimple a dark divot in her cheek and the red lights from the venue's sign bathing her in a head-to-toe blush; washing out the beginnings of a black eye from the elbow she'd taken to her face in the mosh pit. Minoo couldn't feel a thing, though. Her body still tingled. And Kit, uncharacteristically subdued and dreamy—quietly echoed Minoo's sentiment:

"Yeah, it was great, Cala." She laced her fingers through Minoo's.

They held hands all the way home, Kit inching as close to Minoo as her seatbelt allowed, fingers tracing the underbelly of Minoo's forearm, and Minoo felt a fluttering lightness at the perfect loneliness of skyscrapers with only a few lights on, at the taillights of the other cars, illuminating a candied trail out of the city. At the pitch of night as they moved closer to home; a sky that finally revealed itself, full-bellied, stuffed with stars. Minoo relaxed back against the seat and allowed her head to roll from the window to Kit. At first, Minoo thought she was sleeping, but then Kit smiled, as if sensing eyes on her. Gently, she tugged Minoo toward her and kissed the corner of her mouth.

"A kiss?" I squeaked into the darkness under the comforter.

I can feel Minoo nod her head.

A kiss, and also, Minoo revealed, what happened at the concert. In the mosh pit. Covered in other people's sweat and spitting distance from the front of the stage and the amps and the bass reverberating through her guts and the lead singer's voice, tearing out of the speakers and into her bones. Minoo couldn't have predicted the way bodies would become so frenetic they'd vibrate out of themselves, out of their ability to feel the bodies around them. She watched heads slam into other heads and elbows into stomachs and knees into backs. When the set began, Kit and Minoo jumped around with the rest of the audience, their hair whipping around their heads and laughter lost to music. But soon, as the energy and audience grew, Kit and Minoo became pinned between the weight of the crowd and the metal gates separating the audience from the stage. Minoo caught an elbow in the eye, and a large body came crashing down on Kit, driving her head into the metal rail. There was no room to fall to the floor, so when Kit lost consciousness, she did so standing up, her head drooped forward and body swaying with the other bodies around them.

Though it was impossible to act right away, at no point was Minoo paralyzed about what she needed to do. She just wasn't sure how she could do it. Loud as it was; limited as her movements were against the wall, people behind her. The answer came in the form of a body dropping over the edge of the crowd to her left and into the space between the barricade and the stage. Then another to her right. And then another. A swarm of security guards appeared and began to usher the crowd surfers around the ends of the gates and back into the crowd. Minoo reached out and grabbed one of the guards by the sleeve—by what she could grab of the sleeve, his arm bulging against the stiff polyester of his uniform. He turned, his eyes like train tunnels, boring into her face, but she didn't let go. Snaking her other arm around Kit's waist, she pushed Kit in front of her and mouthed, *please.* Within seconds, the guard dragged them both over the gate and a moment later, deposited them in a small, dimly lit office at the very back of the venue. It was cooler there. Quieter. Kit started to come around, her eyelashes fluttering open.

The security guard glared at them, opening his mouth to say something, then clamped it shut. He took a deep breath. "You've gotta be more careful in the pit." The girls nodded. Then, pointing to Kit. "And you might want to get that head checked out."

He left, shutting the door behind him.

The sound of the concert dimmed; became a distant sea. They looked around. A sagging maroon couch was pushed up against the back wall. A large desk on wheels, with one wheel missing, slouched in the centre of the room. On it were boxes of lightbulbs and sponges. A loose stack of flyers. A coffee mug with a deep purple lipstick print. A stapler and roll of masking tape. Minoo focused on these things. Tried to work the whoosh of her rushing pulse out of her ears.

"Minoo?"

Minoo turned to Kit, who was standing with her fingers resting gingerly on her jaw. She spit something into her palm. They looked down. A tooth. A bloody tooth. A molar, it looked like. The right side of her face had a thick red line from the corner of her mouth to the lobe of her ear, where her head had hit the guardrail.

Kit's eyes were clear but distant. "This feeling," Kit began then trailed off. "You know how when you're a kid, and you lost a tooth, there was that strange feeling of absence for a while?" She poked around in her mouth with her tongue.

Minoo nodded.

"But eventually you get used to it." Blood trickled from the corner of her mouth. Her tongue flicked out, licked it. "That absence."

Kit's lips—they glistened slick red.

And her irises, not blue like the sky but blue like the sky reflected in water, they deepened.

There was no thought when their mouths met, and who's to say whose met whose first? There was only the gravity of bodies pulling toward each other.

"You lost a button," Cala said when she and Judith pulled up to the curb outside the club. Cala pointed out her open window. "There, the top button." Minoo looked down at her vest, her hair, now wild again, covering her blooming bruise. There were two strands of thread where the button used to be. Minoo clutched the empty space and looked frantically around her on the sidewalk, spinning in a circle.

"It's not a big deal, azizam," Cala chuckled. "Just pointing it out in case you want to sew on a new one sometime. Now get in the car you two."

Under the covers that night, the memory of hands in hair, on warm skin, on ribs, hips, under waistbands. The metallic tang of Kit's blood and the heat of Kit's body and the catch in her breath and the sternum-splitting knowledge they would never be close enough. Not even if Minoo was stitched into Kit's body and could live there. Even then, it would not be enough. Not ever.

Not ever had she felt like that before.

Not ever would she again. This is something we know now. Atanas, for all Minoo's love of him, never inspired urgency. Only acceptance. This is a good thing. As we grew older, especially, I reminded Minoo how good this thing is: unquestioning, unflinching acceptance. When I say this, she nods along. She understands. She agrees; with all her heart, she knows Atanas is who she needs now. But when you are young, you're driven by thirst. And Kit was the ocean. And Kit was everywhere, and undrinkable.

That night, all Minoo knew was Kit. Shame would come later.

It always did.

"So," I whispered from the black tent of duvet. "Did she taste like ice cream?"

SHOW ME WHERE THE PUPPET HURT YOU...

Minoo leaves me sprawled on my back across the passenger seat when she stops to get gas. We've learned that fuel fumes easily impregnate my fibres. And you never know what someone has on their hand when they pump gas. The last time I pumped, my mouth became coated in a brackish goo that Minoo had to spot-clean with peroxide when we got home, machine washing being out of the question, my parts being as precariously put together as they are.

"People are filthy," I mimicked Minoo's mother's voice, adding to its shrill edge for comedic effect. Minoo let a giggle burst inside her mouth. It's soothing, you see: to accept that the nonsense of this life is the only thing that really matters. That in the end, the only thing we'll care to remember are the moments of lightness: a blanket of lemony sunshine across the wall of your childhood bedroom. The press of your lips into the soft crook of your baby's arm. The great, greedy blue sky you walked under, hand in hand, with the first person you loved.

There's a metallic clunk as Minoo inserts the nozzle into the fuel filler. The tank is not even half empty, but as we move closer to home, Minoo is realizing she's in no rush to get there. She has anticipated the thud of the solid oak front door shutting behind her. The oblongs of sunshine spilling through the sidelights, illuminating dusty floorboards.

The faded brilliance of the hardwood.

The weight of the quiet.

The foyer unfolding into the dining room on her right, then, a little further down the hall, the kitchen.

The stairs directly ahead, ascending into the lethargy of late afternoon. The upstairs's powdery scent of talcum.

And on her left, the creased leather comfort of the family room and its bronze-plated chess table. Atanas's Zenith radio. The spinning wheel coffee table. The familiar books on the bookshelves.

But none of her creations. Not anymore.

All of us—all except me—are wrapped in tissue paper and packed away in a small storage bin in the upstairs closet between the bathroom and Minoo's old room. Now Roya's room. Roya's old room. Twenty-one in total of my wool and cotton and synthetic brethren, buried under spare comforters, sleeping bags, a tent, tennis rackets, Roya's ice skates and skis, cobwebs and darkness. Minoo had packed them away quietly after Roya called us an infestation. Their absence depresses me a little, if I'm being honest. I miss their silly faces. Miss how the absurdity of their existence legitimized my own.

I'm lonely.

I'll say it.

I'll say it because she won't.

I'm lonely even though I'm never alone. Even when we're not together, we are. Because I know everything, remember?

Everything she knows. Everything she's ever thought or experienced, without her having to tell me.

She usually wants to tell me anyway. She needs to. Because saying something out loud makes it easier to bear. Helps you see your thoughts in front of you, ill-formed and writhing like worms that need to be poked and prodded into something with which you can live. This, of course, does not always mean that what you're looking at is the truth. Only what you can accept.

I'll say it because she won't:

We're lonely.

Minoo didn't want to name the rest of the puppets, but I named them all. The purple cat with cross-stitched eyes, copper wire whiskers, and foam ears. It used to sit beside Atanas's grandmother's fancy Royal Albert plates on the shelves of the kitchen hutch. I called her Colette.

Tinker was a cow made from one of Atanas's gym socks. Using permanent black marker, Minoo coloured black spots on the white cotton and sewed two black half-shank buttons in place as eyes. She repurposed a yellow gingham baby bow of Roya's and fastened it between Tinker's floppy black velvet ears. Her nose was fashioned from fuzzy pink wool felt, with two dainty nostrils markered in place. Tinker was quiet and gentle, and easily distracted by the smell of old paper and rainbow prisms cast through windows. Which happened frequently, since she spent her time on the bookshelf in the family room. If it hadn't been for this, I feel she would have been a better companion for Minoo—a more sympathetic listener than me. Something about the uncomplicated set of her mouth.

Fin was an intersex merperson with the bones from an actual fishtail stitched down the front of a green stocking. Minoo bleached the bones after dinner one night and left it to dry before sewing it in place, then surrounding it with dozens of navy and coral stick-on rhinestones. Fin had an orange seashell over their breast and steel wool hot glued to their face to create a fierce and magnificent beard, and to their chest to create some chest hair too. They also had a small bronze starfish glued like a stylish mole over one side of their mouth—the side Minoo had markered a pouting, hypothermic purple. Their long hair, fashioned from hundreds of strands of embroidery floss, was a kaleidoscope of undersea colours: greys, blues, greens, and blacks. Golds and silvers. Minoo spent days on the hair, threading and tying each length into Fin's scalp individually. Their elegance made them perfectly suited to bathe in the temperate, golden halo cast by the light fixture above the dining room table.

The blue elephant—I called him Peanut. For years he remained on top of the medicine cabinet in the upstairs bathroom, growing dim with dust, but standing as a constant, familiar face to greet Minoo in the morning. In the middle of the night. Before bed, reminding Minoo to floss her teeth. In the afternoon when she needed to splash cold water on her face after Roya came home from school, fifteen years old and furious with her mother for driving down main street with me on her hand in plain sight, blaring Queen and singing loudly.

"It's mortifying, Mom! My friends already thought you were weird but now they think you're crazy! Do you have any idea how hard it is to be a teenager with a mother like you?"

"Roya," I intervened, "I know you're upset…"

Roya shoved me out of her face. "MOM!" Roya's cheeks flamed. "I don't want to talk to a fucking puppet! This isn't a game!"

Minoo turned to me, pleading, her dark eyebrows stitching together. But I knew when to shut up. I looked away.

Roya dropped her book bag on the floor, her body deflating. "I just want to talk to my mother." Her voice became threadbare. "My mother, Mom." She kicked at her bag. "Whoever that is." A deep breath. "I don't think you know either." Roya glued her clear gaze to Minoo's and spoke quietly, but firmly. "I mean, what about my brother?"

Her brother.

Maybe Roya was right: Minoo didn't know who she was. She'd created me—all of us—to help her make sense of herself. We have always been an expression of feeling she could not otherwise articulate, or curiosity she couldn't let herself otherwise explore: playfulness, sexiness, authority. And at first, we were helpful. I like to think I was mostly helpful at first, anyway. Now, I am not so sure. I've seen Minoo live for the few moments after a new puppet's completion, when she'd turn a bright new face to hers, witness its first button-eyed blink into existence. In that moment, Minoo was overcome by joy. Possibilities.

Possibilities that were never ours to make happen.

That same afternoon in the bathroom, patting the cool water off her face with a downy hand towel, Minoo looked at her blue elephant peering at her from the summit of the medicine cabinet and time passed at dew speed: slick and slow. Roya's face when she'd said those words, so like her own face, looking at her own mother, so many times. Not angry. Eyes wide. Jaw slack. Desperate.

Minoo had spent years trying to get her mother to talk to her; her father as well, to a lesser extent. From the time she'd arrived in Canada, Minoo called home weekly and spoke to her mother each time, which, of course, is not the same as really talking. Her mother was only interested in how Minoo was doing in school and since Minoo always did well in school, in all subjects, there was never much to report. Her mother still found something to criticize though, so she latched on to Minoo's love of theatre.

"Allah gave you intelligence and you insist on being ridiculous to spite me. There is no future in the arts."

"I'm sure your mother loves you," Kit had soothed when Minoo confided in her about the conversation—a conversation that still left Minoo with the familiar, sternum-splitting pressure in her chest. Their bodies were pressed together in the cocoon of Cala's backyard hammock. Sunlight dripped through the leaves of the large twin maples that flanked the hammock and dappled their thighs. "But my mom has always said that not all love is good for us. And no love means you're free to demand as much as you want from someone." Kit began swaying, so the hammock gently swayed too. Starlings chittered in the branches. "Your mom doesn't get to send you away and keep you close too. She can't have it both ways." The hammock continued to rock and Minoo felt Kit's tapered fingers slip between her own. In the heady buzz of August, katydids purred in the garden.

Minoo loves her kids without condition, but also maybe, without intention. Unconditional love without intention can also be love without accountability. A sort of wishy-washy excuse for doing everything for someone, except what you don't think you're capable of doing. Like convincing yourself that your son is better off without you. Like convincing yourself that because your daughter is strong—stronger than you ever were—she isn't still vulnerable. She doesn't still need you too.

In Minoo's mind, when she thinks of her children together—when she tries to picture their faces as she remembers them best—they are both still so young, their faces flushed and happy, with cheeks so round she could lose her lips in kissing them. When she thinks of them, they are always laughing, and in this suspended past-state, it's easy to miss the fact that now, maybe they're not.

Roya's question: What about my brother?

Minoo didn't wait years to try to contact him directly due to a lack of love or because she didn't have a physical longing for him, something she didn't understand but which made her split and splinter again and again and again. She didn't reach out to him at first because she was a child too, and she'd needed her mother more.

Minoo gets back into the car after paying for the gas, buckles her seat belt, and starts the engine, but we don't move. Instead, she flexes her fingers and considers my form on the passenger seat carefully. To her mind, I look less sprawled in relaxation, as I did when she got out of the car, and more puddled in defeat. My mouth is unhinged. My head, thrown back as if I've been shot. She reaches toward me, then pulls back, tapping her fingers against her chin and gnawing on the inside of her cheek.

I look pathetic, I know, and this isn't helping her sort things out. It endears me to her more. This isn't my intention. My wool, she's sure, is losing colour, right before her eyes. My grey fading to dingy white. My little red tongue bleeding to an anemic pink. Minoo reaches over to the passenger seat and picks me up. She slips me over her hand, slowly. Turning to face one another, we sigh.

THE NATURE OF COLLECTIVE LONGING

Years ago, when Minoo first arrived in Canada, she found her new home cold, even in late May. She grew accustomed to the climate, eventually, but at that moment she huddled between Cala and Judith on the front porch swing, ensconced in their warmth and the purple and silver winter ski suit and matching mittens her mother had packed in her suitcase before she left. Judith's long legs stretched out in front of them. Bare and freckled. The rich, nutty scent of coffee steaming from the cup in her lap. Cala, in a sky-blue cotton sundress, had wrapped an arm around Minoo's shoulder and was stroking her hair with the absent-minded fondness that Minoo would learn was part of who she was: someone with whom affection was unpractised and love itself didn't need to be earned to be shown.

Mrs Beswick sat diagonally across from them in the wicker rocking chair, tucked into the corner of the porch railing under a hanging fern with well-fed cnidarian's limbs unfurling from its straw basket. The ice in her nearly empty gin and tonic melted in her glass on the small, round bistro table to her right. Mrs Beswick had kicked off her sandals and was gently rocking herself with a big toe. She was telling a story Ed, her husband, had told her years ago. They had only been married fifteen months before he died at work. He was a mechanic, and the box of a dump truck he was working on crushed him when the hydraulics failed. This is not the story Mrs Beswick was telling at the time. She had told Minoo that story shortly after they met, after Minoo asked where her husband was. The question was natural enough: Mrs Beswick was a missus, after all. But Minoo knew she'd said something wrong the moment she saw Mrs Beswick's face twitch, as if she'd been slapped. She recovered her expression quickly, but Minoo looked down at her hands and willed herself to disappear.

Mrs Beswick's hand appeared on one of her own. Slender, creamy, but also thickly blue-veined; a hand used to holding on to things tightly.

"No." She lifted Minoo's face to hers with a finger. "You said nothing wrong. Nothing to feel bad for. It's an honest question. A good question. Good questions can just sometimes be sad questions too." Mrs Beswick smiled, her eyes shining. "But that shouldn't stop you from asking them."

The dinner they had just finished was in honour of Mr and Mrs Beswick's wedding anniversary. It would have been their thirtieth, Cala informed Minoo while preparing the dinner earlier that day. Juje—saffron chicken with basmati rice.

"Well, I guess it still is their thirtieth." Cala wiped a loose strand of hair out of her face with the back of her wrist, then went back to placing thick chunks of raw meat into the saffron and garlic marinade. "It's not like they agreed to stop being married."

The stories started at the kitchen table shortly after Mrs Beswick's last sip of her first drink. She talked about her wedding day, the large ceremony that she hadn't wanted but her husband's family insisted she have. About a girl she knew when she was younger—a little older than her in school, the sister of one of her friends—who'd gotten pregnant and hung herself in her father's barn. When her parents cut her down, they found burn marks on her palms. She'd tried to pull herself back up the rope. She'd tried to stop what she started. She'd changed her mind. Mrs Beswick talked about the oatmeal cookies her grandmother used to give her when she came to visit, and how they tasted like her grandfather's pipe smoke. The walls of the house were yellowed with it. Mrs Beswick told them about a young man she'd seen on a street in Toronto once. She was nineteen, and when they'd passed each other on the sidewalk, they'd both turned to look at each other. He'd smiled, the most beautiful smile she'd ever seen—lupine, paired with puppy eyes—and her friends dragged her on, into the crowd, but she still thinks of that young man all the time.

"I'm sure he would've been the ruin of me." Mrs Beswick waved her hand, grinning.

By the time the four of them moved to the porch for coffee (for Cala and Judith) and another drink (for Mrs Beswick), and Mrs Beswick was rocking herself with her toe and telling a new story, Minoo couldn't recall how that story went before it spun off into the next one. Her mind was muddled by a full belly of dinner and the slow warmth from Judith and Cala's bodies on either side of hers, creeping through her snowsuit. But she trusted there was a connection there because Mrs Beswick spoke without hesitation. Without losing her thread.

"The little girl was the youngest of many children," Mrs Beswick continued the story. "I don't remember exactly how many children there were. I think five or six." She waved her hand. "It doesn't really matter. There were a lot of children, that's my point. And this girl, she was five years old, Ed's age at the time. He told me of how, after the girl's mother died, she would cry in the middle of class. Just sit there and bawl for her mother, like a lamb." Mrs Beswick paused her story for a moment to take another sip of her drink. Minoo pictured the little girl, her hungry, wet eyes. Her white dress with puffed sleeves, milky skin, and pink ribbons fastening curled, blonde pigtails. "Eventually," Mrs Beswick began again, putting her glass back on the table and smoothing her cotton skirt over her narrow hips, "the teacher learned that the child wouldn't stop until each and every one of her siblings was retrieved from their class and brought to comfort her. The image of that poor child crying," she shakes her head. "Of all those children, huddled together on the classroom floor..." Mrs Beswick's eyelids blinked slowly over watery eyes. "Well, Ed said it haunted him all his life."

Minoo pictured the girl alone, like a crumpled tissue. Her pale little face and whirlpool eyes. Imagined the girl's classmates and a pudding-chinned teacher circling her at a distance. As if her grief was contagious. Because grief is contagious. Every loss is a reminder of your potential for it.

Minoo remembered her mother's hand enveloping her smaller one as they crossed the street. The feel of it. Gentle. For a time, life had been so gentle. Gentle as her lips on the mid-leg fold of her baby's thigh. She could feel the warmth of their faces pressed together, cheek to cheek, in sleep.

Her baby.

The way we are gifted these moments for the short time we are small and soft and good enough to deserve them.

"It was so long ago now." Mrs Beswick murmured into her drink. A sad smile melted its way across her face. Cala squeezed Minoo to her side and kissed the top of her head.

Judith rubbed her arm. And somewhere in the depths of this warmth, Minoo registered a familiar ache.

Minoo checks her phone before putting the car in drive to continue on our way home. Nothing from Atanas or Roya. There's the email from Cala she got last night, letting her know she and Judith would be down for a visit in a week, but no new messages. She checks spam. No. No email at all. We've been trying to distract her from this: the compulsive checking for a response to the email she sent a week ago. Nine days ago, actually.

An email to her son.

She clicks on her sent email, just to make sure the message really was sent, and to the right address. Even though she'd already checked this yesterday. And the day before. And the day before that.

It's been almost a month since Darius contacted her. Until then, Minoo had not seen or heard from him since Gilan. He'd searched her name, he explained, assuming that, like most Iranian women, she wouldn't have changed her last name. Eventually, he found her picture and email address on a long-forgotten Facebook page for a now-defunct local dance studio where Roya had taken ballet classes. For the seven years Roya danced, Minoo had been enlisted as a volunteer to help sew costumes—mostly simple tulle tutus adorned with small pearl beads or polyester flowers—and her email address had been provided for parents to contact her with their children's measurements.

After reading his email, Minoo had gone straight to the studio's Facebook page. The last post announced the studio's closing. May 14, 2015. The owner and sole teacher, Mrs Purdy, was retiring after forty-five years of instruction, the post explained. Minoo still runs into her around town from time to time; her posture, still unflinching and impeccable in her eighties.

"Headlights on the balcony, Ms Minoo!" Mrs Purdy hollers whenever she sees her, across the produce aisle or street or coffee shop. Minoo, who is inevitably slouching, always snaps her spine straight and dutifully executes an off-balance curtsy.

Minoo found the post Darius referred to after a few minutes of scrolling. Just as he said, there was her name, her email, and a picture of Roya wrapping her in yards of pink and purple tulle, straight-jacket style. In the photo, Roya wore a black leotard that emphasized her bird-boned body. She was leaning back, pulling the tulle tight with the full weight of her ten years. Minoo's hair was gathered into a frantic top knot, curls springing loose from her head. They both smiled gamely at the camera.

Minoo zoomed in on Roya's face. Her smile was full, lighting the green of eyes. Her hair—long then, down to her waist—was braided and wrapped about her head in a crown. How many hours had Minoo spent with her hands buried in her daughter's hair? She could still feel its silken mass between her fingers.

I found him, Darius had written, and Minoo knew who he meant. *We've spoken. He's well and happy and open to hearing from you, if you're interested. I've included his email below.*

She started drafting an email within minutes of finishing Darius's, but it took us awhile to get it right. And when we hit send, we checked and double-checked that the email went out, just as we made sure, multiple times, that Minoo had typed the email address correctly.

"Minoo," I say. "It hasn't even been that long. And it wasn't exactly a run-of-the-mill 'Hey, how are ya' sort of email. He probably needs time to process. Darius said he didn't get back to him right away either."

She ignores me, continuing to stare at the screen.

"I'm just saying, you dropped some heavy stuff."

She's staring down at her phone, reconsidering her subject line:

> Subject: I guess you could call this an introduction...

She had been trying to be breezy with that line. To not sound desperate or crazy. But—Minoo's head jerks up, her throat choked—it might have sounded like spam. Like a Nigerian prince. Or some solicitous Russian mail-order bride. I suggested she get Atanas's help with the letter—he was always so good at saying the right thing—but Minoo said she wasn't going to tell him about anything, not Darius reaching out, and not about the letter, unless there was something to really tell. She insisted that nothing had actually changed, even though, of course, so much had. Now, there was hope. Real hope.

Minoo was prepared to be rejected, but only privately. She couldn't have it happen with Atanas's knowledge.

Rereading the subject line again, Minoo's pulse pounds in her wrist. She continues.

> Dear Davood,
> I'm happy (and nervous!) to be writing to you.
> It's taken too long, I know.

"You must know this email by heart, by now."

Minoo flicks me a side eye, then resumes looking at the screen.

"I know I do." Minoo's Farsi is rusty, since she only speaks it on the rare occasions her mother answers the phone, and being out of practice has compounded her anxiety that she might not have found the right words. It meant we reread the email countless times before it was sent. I begin to recite the next words from the email: "You already know of me, I believe. Darius found me after he reached out to you, and informed me that he told you everything. I'm glad you are going to meet him in a few months."

Darius had been married for fourteen years. He'd met his wife in California, which is where he settled after dropping out of medical school in Toronto. Minoo wishes she had known at the time; it might have helped to know he was so near.

"Yeah, I was sent away to live with family too," he explained over WhatsApp video. He and Minoo had decided to move platforms after exchanging a few emails, sensing, both of them it seemed, that their old understanding—their easy acceptance—of one another was still there. "A few months after you left. Not sure what changed. One minute I'm at home reading comics and the next I'm at the airport being told I'm going to Ontario to stay with some relative I've barely heard of." Darius chuckles, rubbing the back of his neck. "It's like the diaspora exists only to send money home, and to house wayward kids."

He paced what Minoo assumed was his backyard. The sunlight behind him cast his face mostly in shadow, but his smile was clear. Radiant. Just as she remembered. She remembered how he made her feel: so absorbed by his ease in his own body that she became unconcerned with her own. She beamed.

"To think," he adds. "If our mothers had ever bothered to speak again after you left, they would have learned they exiled their children to the same place."

Darius now works as a private airline pilot. "Of all things," he laughed, and the sound was just sweetly playful as she remembered. "Being Iranian and trusted to fly a plane in this country is no small feat."

He said he'd told his wife about Minoo and the baby long ago. "A few weeks after we met, actually. She encouraged me to find him. To find you. She has always been supportive. I mean, I just want to make sure you know that me finding him now has nothing to do with she and I not being able to have kids of our own. I don't want you to think that. She wanted me to reach out to you both before we knew we couldn't…" he rubbed the back of his neck, his eyes slipping from hers. "Anyway."

Darius stopped walking and sat down. Behind him, Minoo could see a tall, wooden fence stained golden brown. A large planter brimming with what looked like a lemon tree. And, very clearly, a fig tree. Just like they'd had at his home. In this new position, only half of his face was obscured by shadow, cast by what Minoo imagined—judging by how his face was divided diagonally from opposite temple to jaw—must be a patio table umbrella. From somewhere near his feet, a small dog yipped. One of his shoulders dropped, presumably to pet it.

"I was looking for you too," he continued, looking down at the dog. "I just found him first."

Him. Neither of them had called him their son yet. They'd even been using his name sparingly; protectively. As if, if they used it too much, they'd wear it thin. It would disappear. He might disappear.

"An old school friend who lives in Tehran managed to track him down." Darius brought the dog up onto his lap. A diminutive breed, with gleaming button black eyes, a teddy bear nose, pointy ears, and fine, longish hair, the colour of nougat and caramel. Minoo, who was sitting at the kitchen table, sipped at her tea.

"I knew who your parents were, so it wasn't too hard. My friend is familiar with the neighbourhood your parents lived in, and after asking around, found out that your dad plays chess in the park most Friday afternoons. I remember him playing with my dad on the few occasions he came to visit. You remember?"

Minoo nodded. The dog had a little pink tongue that stuck out the side of its mouth. Minoo glanced across the table to where she'd placed me on my bottle—close enough for comfort, but out of sight. My fuzzy tongue poked out too.

"So, he went there, and since your dad was a fairly well-known regular, found him easily enough and asked him to play. The rest is history. Your dad was pretty open about Davood. Probably because Reza—that's my friend—didn't say anything about me or indicate that he knew who your dad was. They just talked about life. That sort of thing. Your dad told him what he needed to know."

Darius's gaze moved over the screen. He was looking at something or no, someone, behind his device, because he smiled and nodded before returning his attention to Minoo.

"He's working at an engineering firm now. Still lives with your parents but has friends who keep him out of the house most nights. Your dad seems to think well of them. His friends, I mean, though he indicated your mom wasn't so happy about his social life." They both chuckled. Minoo could imagine her mother wouldn't be. Out meant up to no good, no doubt. But it was still more freedom than she was ever allowed. Darius scratched the dog behind its ears and in return, the small animal pressed its head into his hand, eyes closed and chin lifted in pure elation.

"It was only when I connected with him that I learned about you." Minoo brought her attention back to his face. "That you'd been separated."

Minoo nodded, a gesture that might have signified pre-existing knowledge of a fact that was actually totally new to her: Davood did know she existed. When her mother had said otherwise she'd been lying. Or, she was telling the truth and her son had somehow found out later. He knew what Minoo was to him. And him to her. Blood rushed to her ears. Static in her chest. We locked eyes across the kitchen. I knew it and she knew it: She had to reach out to him.

"It's not that I didn't care," Darius went on. Minoo blinked. The dog had disappeared from his lap, and now his face was closer to the screen. A good face. His gently lined forehead. Bottom lashes so thick it looked like he was wearing eyeliner. A bluish shadow of stubble sweeping up his jaw. The cleft in his chin, the size of the pad of a baby's toe.

"I just," Darius dropped his chin to his chest, then lifted his head again, exhaling heavily through his mouth. "I was just a kid. A really fucking dumb kid. I didn't know what to do. I'm sorry." Before Minoo can say anything, like *I'm sorry too*, or *there's nothing to be sorry for*, the dog barked again from somewhere under the table. Darius bent down to pick up the animal and knocked the table with his head. He swore and his phone slid onto its back, screen up to reveal the great, gaping sky.

Minoo closes her eyes. I've stopped reciting the email out loud, but the next words Minoo wrote are in my head.

I'm glad he contacted you. I'm also sorry I wasn't the one to do it. I should have, years ago.

In the email, Minoo had been careful not to call Darius his father. Or herself his mother. He probably wouldn't think of them that way. She referred to him as her child, sometimes, privately, but tried not to call him that out loud. She had no right, she thought. She'd called him your brother when she used to speak about him to Roya, but she felt she had no right to call him her anything.

Strange, maybe, that Minoo never realized this limitation of language until she wrote that email. Until she was forced to position herself to him in writing and her feelings were forced to take shape outside her head. When you are thinking of someone, after all, your emotions are real but amorphous. Until you need to externalize them though, then there's no saving yourself from their weight.

"Minoo!" Minoo jumps in her seat. I'm not yelling, exactly, but I am speaking loudly. Directly into her ear. She turns her face to me so we're nose to nose.

"This isn't helping," Minoo's eyes narrow.

"Drive home."

> Davood, I was always waiting for permission to reach out to you. I know now that I needed no permission, and I have no excuse. I am an adult and have been for a long time. You are an adult too now, and I think that even now, my reaching out to you directly won't be approved of, but there is really no one to stop us from speaking. If you want to.
>
> I've missed you.
>
> I don't want to overwhelm you, so I'll leave off here.
>
> I hope to hear from you as soon as you feel ready, whenever that is.
>
> Affectionately,
>
> M

YOUNG LOVE IS LIKE A SUGAR CUBE

Minoo pulled aside the curtain and peeked out at the audience. She spotted Kit within seconds, seated beside Cala. Third row. Kit's hair was slicked back, darkened by gel to a coppery blonde. She wore red lipstick that looked like it was going to melt the mouth off her face, and a strapless black velvet top.

Kit was in her school auditorium. Minoo blinked. Blinked again.

Kit holding a bouquet of roses in her arms. Yellow. Minoo's favourite colour.

Kit leaning toward Cala to better hear some silly joke. They were both laughing and Minoo felt the opening-night tension unravel in her body. Kit. A whole world in one syllable.

This was Minoo's second performance with her school drama club. After *Alice in Wonderland* last school year, she'd been cast again, this time as another Alice. Alice Sycamore—the lead in their spring performance of *You Can't Take It with You.*

"It's a play about love conquering class divides. Love conquering all," Minoo heard Cala explain to Minoo's mother on the phone one morning. "It's not nonsense. It's bringing Minoo out of her shell." Minoo was late for school, so she couldn't guess at her mother's response from what Cala said next, but as she shut the front door behind her, she could imagine it.

Minoo doesn't need to come out of her shell. She needs to get back in it, for the sake of us all!

For the sake of us all, just disappear.

And Minoo was. She was disappearing into someone else: quirky and loveable Alice Sycamore with her eccentric, affectionate, and accepting family.

She had not bothered to tell her mother about the specifics of the play this time because she already knew that her mother disapproved of her being in plays at all. She did email her mother a picture of her after the show, though. It was taken backstage, where Kit and Cala had rushed after the performance. Kit had thrown her arms around Minoo, the cellophane wrapping of the roses crinkling behind her head.

"You were brilliant!" Kit pulled back just enough to beam into Minoo's face but still hold her. "That line: 'I'm sick of cornflakes!' I'm so proud of you!"

In the picture, Minoo was grinning so wide her face looked like it would shatter. There was such joy in that moment. Such was her love for Kit, who'd pulled her close, and Cala, who took the picture of them like that, arms wrapped around each other, bouquet hanging upside down against Minoo's back.

"Who's this girl?" Her mother's voice was clenched. Like she was trying not to belch. Or vomit. "In the picture, with the jendeh lipstick and naked arms?"

Minoo shifted from foot to foot in the kitchen, winding and unwinding the phone cord around a finger.

"A friend?" Her mother snorted. "Why is she looking at you like that? Like a sugar cube."

Minoo ground her teeth.

"There's something wrong with her. Fahesheh. She looks sticky. Someone needs to take a hose and horse brush to her."

Minoo pictured Kit's skin—ivory and smooth—scrubbed pink by her mother's rough hands.

"Disgusting," her mother clucked.

Minoo was never so ashamed of who she was until she saw herself through the eyes of her mother, and still, even today, she sees herself that way most of the time.

A few months later, Kit announced she was moving to BC with her mom and her mom's new boyfriend, and Minoo's world collapsed.

"It's not like I really have a choice." Kit shrugged. They were on the swings at the park near the centre. They hadn't been to classes in almost a year, but the park was close to the mall with the wishing fountain, the bus stop, and their favourite convenience store that let you add gummies to the Slurpees for only fifty cents more. It was part of their history. It made sense that Kit would break the news there.

That afternoon, the park was almost empty, except for a man eating a sandwich with his poodle. For every bite he took, he broke off a little piece for the dog.

"And he's not a bad person." Kit spoke of the boyfriend. "I mean, my mom's the one who got the promotion and has to move. He's leaving everything behind for us. Well, for my mom. I guess I can respect that." Kit dragged her sneakers over the pebbles at her feet. Minoo didn't know what Kit's mother did for work. Or, more likely, she was told and promptly forgot, the lives of most adults being unimportant to children. Whatever it was, it was taking Kit away.

"Anyway..." Kit began pumping her legs again, the skirt of her floral sundress licking at her thighs.

The night of the concert was never replicated. Their intimacy. No, not intimacy. The word made Minoo recoil, thinking of the smell of dark, wet places. Places that she knew had nothing to do with Kit did not remind her of Kit one bit—but reminded her of herself. Her mother's stern, unsmiling face. The metallic funk of an old sanitary napkin her mother once found wrapped, but reeking, behind the wastebasket in their bathroom. She'd dragged Minoo into the bathroom by her braid, then pulled her down to her knees, pointing to the shrouded bundle, hissing, "Filthy. You filthy girl."

Minoo had just started her period that day. Was still wearing the first pad she'd had to use. And her pads were wrapped in pink. The wad behind the basket was wrapped in purple. It couldn't have been hers. But her mother had pinned her to the floor by her braid, on level with the gag-rot of old blood, so she held her breath instead of arguing. She picked the old pad up, put it in a plastic bag, and took the bag to the fly-swarmed trash can outside, just as her mother told her.

Minoo started swinging again too, building momentum until she was falling back as Kit hurtled forward. Their experience the night of the concert had not been repeated but it had not been entirely ignored, either. When they stayed over at each other's houses, they fell asleep on their sides, face to face, hands clasped, lips close. When they saw each other after any measure of time apart, they had to touch before they spoke, slipping arms around waists, under shirts. Skin to skin. Or pressing foreheads together, eyes closed.

Kit would promise, her fingers traveling up the back of Minoo's shirt, tracing delicate patterns. "I can wait."

"I can wait," Kit said again, whipping past on the swing, a blur.

Minoo pumped harder, body jackknifing the sky, feeling as if her stomach were spilling open.

After six months of Kit's absence, Minoo stopped returning her calls or replying to her emails. Concerned, Cala prodded. Gently at first.

"You're best friends, joonam. Talk to her."

Instead, Minoo talked to me, as she had more and increasingly often after Kit left. She would rather have talked to Kit, but Kit wasn't there anymore. Here's the thing: she wasn't looking for a way out of the way she felt. She simply didn't know how to fight to stay in. She had never learned to fight for the people she cared about. From a very young age, she'd never seen the people she cared about fight for her. At least, not for the person she was, only for the person they wanted her to be.

Eventually Kit stopped calling. Stopped emailing. A few times over the years, Minoo thought about reaching out to her—it would be easy enough to try. Just crack open a laptop. Type in the name. Press enter. But she doesn't. If Kit had wanted to contact her, she would have by now. This is what she reasoned.

"True," I'd say, repeating the same script as last time. "But you were the one who broke off contact with her. If someone should reach out, it should be you." I'd say this, but even I—who was created specifically to give voice to the things Minoo could not—didn't speak the truth. Here's the thing: Minoo used to think her longing was all about Kit. Was about Kit's curves and earthy softness. Her kindness.

The give of her body. Her joy spark. How she saw so much, so clearly, and with so much certainty. How could Minoo not love her? But Minoo didn't contact Kit, because by contacting her, she would have needed to admit something to herself she was too scared and ashamed to admit. That wherever her desires lay, they did so outside the definitions she'd grown up knowing were acceptable. So, our debates always ended with us pretending Minoo was stonewalled by inaction instead of fear. And really, they may not be the same thing, but they are closely related.

Time passes. It changes things. It warps and distills. Minoo back then still longed for Kit. Minoo now—the Minoo driving home from the hospital, frizzy-haired and distraught—can recognize with dizzying clarity that her continued affection for Kit is not about Kit at all. What Minoo longs for is what Kit represents: a few fleeting moments in her younger life when there were more possibilities than certainties. When she was better able to perceive herself from the inside: a whirl of fireflies, bioluminescent gold and violet light. Bodiless. Formless. Perfectly undefined and free as she's ever been. So, this aching, this heartbreaking, sweat-beading longing, hasn't been about Kit for a very long time. If it ever was, entirely, at least. As curious as Minoo is to know what's become of Kit, she needs her to stay in the past. Some people are touchstones, and us being who we are now depends on them staying as they were then, for better or worse.

I'VE GOT A POROUS, EMPTY FEELING

We pull into the driveway, but Minoo doesn't go inside right away. We sit in the car and observe the house, which looks just as good as when Cala lived there. Maybe even a little better, since every few years, Minoo sands and repaints all the gingerbread and fascia. All the railings and posts and spindles. Atanas replaced the warped front steps for Minoo, too. Minoo has kept up with Cala's gardens, which are giddy with lilies and poppies and hollyhocks. Last year, she added two tipsy pink peony bushes that abut the railing leading up the steps. It's not that Cala left the house to Minoo in ruins—not at all, but Cala was not burdened by needing to prove she deserved this life and her relative freedom, so wasn't bothered by flaking paint or a creaky step.

"You're doing good," I nudge her shoulder. "Look at this place."

The corner of Minoo's mouth lifts. A reluctant grin. We leave the car and begin to circle around to the back of the house, stopping momentarily so Minoo can pull a weed from the flower bed and press her palm to the trunk of the towering front yard ash tree that Roya, as a child, named Willow.

"But it's not a willow tree!" I'd told her, laughing, as Minoo ran her hands through her daughter's long hair. Everything Roya did used to delight us.

"But it has a willow spirit!" Roya countered.

She was right. Especially when it flowers, its white fuzzy blossoms dripping from its thin branches, the ash has the lazy elegance of a willow.

Everything Roya does still delights us. But it scares us too. Scares us more these days, if I'm being honest, because now, the full-blown result of all our years together is clear. Now, the person is formed, all her opinions and beliefs, and there's nothing we can do to change it. It's too late to go back and do things differently. Roya reminds us of the permanence of our actions, and how maybe, we've allowed her to think the outcome is her fault.

Minoo whispers hello to Willow before we move on.

So maybe it's more accurate to say we scare us. The unfixable things we've done.

When we step into the backyard, it is a perfect composition of shadow and light, sun pooling in the centre and giving way to pockets of shade as one orbits to the edges.

"Reminds you, doesn't it?"

Her wedding day. The play of tree boughs, the murmur of summer, the air warm but without weight. Minoo stares at the billowy hydrangeas climbing the shed.

"Minoo?"

Without averting her gaze, she nods once.

A woman who showed up to her wedding—the new girlfriend of one of Atanas's university friends. Neither Atanas nor Minoo had met her before. She stood in the back corner by the shed, her strappy heels, impractical in the grass, slipped off and hooked loosely on a finger. In her other hand, a bubbling flute of champagne. The woman leaned comfortably against her date—Minoo can't remember his name or face exactly. There's a vague impression of a coppery beard. A violet pocket square. Yes, violet. The same colour as the girlfriend's long, flowy dress.

The boyfriend was engaged in an animated conversation with Atanas. His wild gestures jockeyed the date around and caused the champagne to splash out of her glass. But the young woman continued to lean, unfazed, gazing into some unknowable distance beyond all of them, her lips giving into a slight grin; a small, private playmate.

In that moment, Minoo recalled Kit fully, as she had not allowed herself to remember her in years, even when she and Atanas started dating seriously and spoke of their pasts; their families, friends, previous relationships. Minoo had shared everything about her parents and her child. She shared details of her relationship with Kit with an eagerness that surprised her. But she left out the confusion and shame she felt, being still too confused and ashamed to articulate such truths. At least this is the reason she told herself—told me—but we both know it is only a half-truth. The other half: she wasn't, and perhaps would never be, ready to share all the details that made up how she felt about Kit, because relinquishing these excruciating complexities would make Kit less hers.

But she felt comfortable telling Atanas more than she'd thought she'd be comfortable sharing—things she had never even told Cala: about the night of the concert in the mosh pit and her first kiss with Kit. How she'd cried every night for the first year she'd been in Canada, how she missed her home so much. Her mother. Her baby. How it made no sense, since her mother had sent her away and she'd now been separated from her child longer than she'd ever been with him. How she wanted to be angry, but couldn't, because being angry would change nothing. Wouldn't help. Being angry required a level of belief in oneself that Minoo had never had. She told him she just wanted to get on with her life.

She told Atanas all this because there are people in your life whom you know, without doubt, love you, and you can feel it, even if you can't see why.

"You're spectacular," he'd said one evening. They were walking in downtown Toronto after seeing a play starring one of their friends from school. They'd meandered down to the waterfront. The water taxis were taking their final trips to the island. There was the smell of hotdogs and the soft thud on boats bumping into the docks. Minoo had been talking about how Cala had attended every show of every play she'd been in, since high school; how she knew she came out of love and support, but also, Minoo suspected, out of pity.

"Pity?" Atanas said. "What are you talking about? You're an amazing performer. That's why people come to see you."

Minoo rolled her eyes and knocked him gently with her shoulder. No, she was sure that wasn't it. Or all of it. Even your favourite show with your favourite actor gets old if you see it seven times in four days. No, Cala came to all her shows because if she didn't, who would? Minoo had her theatre friends, but they were part of the performances with her. There would be no one for her in the audience if Cala didn't go.

"Did Cala ever say that? Do anything that would make you even think that? You can't count showing up as proof of pity."

Minoo thought about it. Cala had shown up to every performance with flowers and smiles. With cattle whistles and applause. Even during her first performance in university when Minoo was pretty sure she'd never even told Cala about the play, there Cala was, beaming at her from the audience, as if there were no other place in the world to be.

Minoo shook her head.

"That's right," Atanas said. "Because you are spectacular. Everything about you is."

Spectacular.

Minoo giggled when he said the word, pictured herself floating, weightless and alone in a dark universe but exploding with starlight from her fingers and toes, from the ends of her hair. Her eyes, glowing. And she loved that. Loved the way he saw her. Never a spectacle. Just spectacular.

The woman at her wedding: Minoo remembers her hair shimmering, pale as moonlight. Her dreamy smile and the dark forest of her eyes. The distance between herself and the person standing right beside her. It didn't matter what the woman was smiling about. Minoo knew how important it was not to interrupt these moments. Such undiluted joy, and at the expense of absolutely no one.

Minoo runs a finger along her clavicle. She never saw the girlfriend again after that day. And Atanas, as far as she knows, never saw the friend either, their lives forking as the lives of young people tend to do. One moment, you're as close to someone as anyone in the world, and the next, two decades have passed and you don't know where they live. If their parents are still alive. If they still have that girlfriend they brought to your wedding who stood barefoot on the grass in the latticed light, her body pressed to your husband's friend's side, daydreaming some private dream in the heady bloom of hydrangeas and the rumbling laughter of men.

After checking on the water in the bird bath, we fold ourselves into the hammock. The afternoon is cooling. From next door, we can hear Mrs Beswick's cribbage game: every Sunday, 3p.m. She'd invited Minoo to join, but once Minoo understood that cribbage was just a thinly disguised and extended math exercise, she declined to play again.

The sound of laughter bursts through Mrs B's open window. The clattering of a teacup onto a saucer. The Eagles song *Peaceful Easy Feeling* on the radio. As a teenager, Roya would often join the weekly game, learning how to "best the old biddies," as Mrs B quipped, under Mrs B's tutelage. Eventually, she became the reigning winner of their weekly tournaments.

"A cribbage prodigy!" I once teased. "You can't really be your mother's daughter!"

"Clearly," Roya snorted, looking at me directly, something she rarely did anymore. Her nostrils twitched, like something smelled bad. "Clearly because crib requires using logic."

A few nights earlier, Roya had crawled into bed between Minoo and Atanas. Bad dream. They happened less as she got older, or maybe Roya just came to them less, but Minoo knew the signs. Shaking. Rapid breathing. Sweat beading on her daughter's forehead. Minoo pulled Roya close, held her to her chest and stroked her hair as she fell back asleep. She inhaled the green-apple sweetness of Roya's favourite shampoo and snuggled into the darkness. She pictured them floating in their bubble through the star-laced universe. Atanas snoozed on.

The next morning at breakfast though, when Minoo had reached out to tuck Roya's curtain of hair behind her ear so she could see her face—see if she looked well rested—Roya swatted her away without stopping from spooning cereal into her mouth.

Minoo sighed.

And she sighed again, watching Roya, insult delivered, peevishly throw her sweatshirt over her head and fly out the side screen door to Mrs B's weekly game. The door bounced once, twice, and a final time as we watched the girl stalk across the backyard, the pendulum swing of her ponytail mimicking the determination of her stride.

"There's no making sense of it," I said. Minoo continued to stare out the window. "She loves you and she hates you. You know how that is."

Minoo worried her lip with her teeth.

"Besides," I stifled a giggle and tried to deepen my voice into a register of complete seriousness. "She does have a point."

Minoo raised an eyebrow.

"Your logic. It's for shit."

No matter what happened before the card games, Roya usually came back in a better mood. Minoo remarked on this once to Mrs B, and Mrs B had simply nodded. "Good."

"Good how?" I asked. Minoo offered a plate of rosewater gaz—Mrs B's favourite Persian dessert that Minoo tried to have on hand. Mrs B selected a piece of the candy and bit into the chewy round powdery nougat. "What goes on over there?"

"Nothing," Mrs B wiped her mouth with a thumb. "We just talk." She took a sip of tea and sighed with pleasure. "This combination," she nodded to the gaz and tea, "is pure heaven." She nibbled at the gaz again. "But, you know, maybe hearing old people talk about our aches and pains and complaints and the innumerable tragedies of our arthritic lives can remind a younger person to be a little more grateful." She popped the remainder of the treat in her mouth and chewed slowly. "Or maybe," Mrs B glanced fleetingly at me then turned her attention back to the plate of gaz. She smiled at the perfect white round she selected before continuing. "Maybe it's just that we're good listeners," she shrugs. "What do I know?"

When Roya returned from the card game after stomping out of the house, she wrapped her arms around her mother's waist while Minoo was at the sink washing a colander of wax green beans.

"Thank you for the Opal Rose, Mom."

Minoo turned off the tap and searched her mind: Opal Rose? She looked at me, staring blankly at her from the windowsill. I had no idea what the kid was talking about either.

"See?" Roya raised a hand in front of Minoo's face and wiggled her fingers. Her daughter's nails were neatly rounded and painted a silvery pink. The nail polish. Yes. Minoo had seen it at the drug store a few weeks ago and knew Roya would love it. Roya rested her cheek against her mother's back.

Minoo brought Roya's fingers to her lips and kissed each one.

Before Roya left to begin university, Mrs B came over with a gift from the cribbage crew: one thousand dollars and a personalized cribbage board. Engraved into the bottom, the message, "Thanks for keeping us young."

Minoo remembers how Roya had cried and launched herself into Mrs B's arms, almost knocking the older woman over. Mrs B gasped in surprised delight.

"I need to thank everyone," Roya sniffled, wiping her eyes with the sleeve of her sweatshirt. "But I'm leaving before the next game!"

"No thanks necessary, dear," Mrs B smiled, rubbing Roya's back. "At our age, we aren't so keen on goodbyes anyway."

As if Mrs B knew then that Roya wasn't ever moving back home again.

As if everyone understood except Minoo.

"That's bullshit," I say from the snuggly embrace of the hammock, interrupting the silence of Minoo's thoughts. "Don't discredit your own intelligence. You knew how things were with Roya. You just didn't fix it."

Minoo huffs and throws her arm with me on it over the hammock's side.

Here's where we're not being honest: When I was brought along to the hospital today, it wasn't because Minoo thought Roya would have a sentimental change of heart caused by holding her child for the first time. Minoo didn't really think this flood of emotion would compel her daughter to remember all the fun we used to have when life was embroidery-floss fine. She may have hoped for this, but she wasn't actually counting on it. She brought me with her because she wasn't thinking of Roya at all. She was only thinking of herself, and what she needed. She needed a buffer, because she was thinking about the day Davood was born and how, when he was placed in her arms, she'd felt the need to wrap herself back around him; to absorb him back into her body. The incomprehensible joy spiral of those first moments. She was thinking about the last time she kissed him before leaving, pressing her lips to the tender chasm above his belly button, and how he'd erupted in bubbling baby laughter. She promised herself she'd always remember that sound.

And she had.

Minoo was thinking about the email, still unanswered. But I needed no permission, and I have no excuse.

She was thinking of a recent phone conversation with her parents, when her dad said her mother was showing signs of memory loss. "She's forgetting certain things, I should say. But she remembers others from long ago. Stories I've never heard are just tumbling out of her mouth. The other day, she told me… Oh wait a second… Joonam! Come here! Minoo's on the phone!"

Minoo put her cell on speaker and placed it on the kitchen counter. She gazed out the window behind my head into the backyard while she washed her yogurt bowl. The morning was spongy grey. Pouring rain, whereas half an hour before, when she'd gone out to the garden to gather raspberries for her yogurt, it was only drizzling. The leaves of the twin maples shook under the light shower. On the other end of the line, there was the sound of her dad mumbling something, a cupboard door slamming, then her mother's voice, growing more distinct as she moved closer to the phone.

"I had to put the cheese away, give me a minute!" Then, to Minoo and right to the point: "Cala sent pictures from her last visit with you. Your face looks different. There are more angles."

Minoo squeezed her eyes shut and placed the heels of her hands against the counter, pushing her body back so her head hung between her shoulders.

"You're looking old," her mother said. There it was. The insult. "Well, not old, but older."

Minoo opened her eyes. Between her feet was the square of tile with the chip in the corner. The chip had always been there, for as long as she'd lived in the house. "Your face…" Minoo could feel her mother searching for words, something she'd never had to do before, the words always present and ready to attack, like a scorpion tail. "Your face has… lost its softness."

Minoo straightened. She met my eyes.

"You don't look like my baby anymore."

Outside, the downpour had intensified. Rain hit the grass so hard it looked like the earth was spitting up. Minoo slipped me off my bottle and over her hand. Bringing me to her chest, as if cradling me, she began to sway. She exhaled, long and slow.

"But these changes happen to us all," her mother went on. "We get old." A familiar slurping sound on the other end of the line: her mother taking a sip of tea. "Did I ever tell you about how my older sisters used to play hide-and-seek with me? No? Well, we did, and once, I hid under my mother's sewing table. I must have been very young, because we were all still living at home. And I remember, hiding there, among the scraps of fabric my mother had dropped on the floor, I peed myself. I was so excited. I could hear my sisters searching for me. Moosham, moosham! Bia moosham! That's what they called me, because they thought I was small and cute like a mouse, but also, a pest." Minoo's mother laughed, a strangled squeak. Minoo continued to stare at me, and I stared back, my mouth hanging open. In all the stories of her khalehs, her mother had always portrayed them as vile, selfish women.

"Waiting for my sisters, I couldn't help it," Minoo's mother's sigh was one of pure bliss. Minoo thought of how Mrs B's cat would stretch out in the middle of the street on warm summer days, sun-drunk and purring and oblivious to danger or the chiding from Mrs B. "I lost all control. I was so happy."

I tapped Minoo's shoulder. "Ask her to come." I mouthed. "Ask her again to come to meet the baby."

Minoo opened her mouth, as if about to argue then shut it, nodded and extended an invitation.

"Na, baba," her mother replied. "I'm too old for such things, Minoo. Too tired."

Minoo didn't know what such things were. Travel? Babies? Reconnecting with family? Maybe, reconsidering them? She didn't know, but she didn't think about it further because she started to think about her mother's voice. It had been crackling as she spoke, like there was static on the line but there wasn't. It must have been crackling like that for some time, Minoo knew. Not the crackle of allergies or illness, but age.

She's forgetting things. The breaks in her mother's once smooth, controlled voice, created fissures in the stone image Minoo had of her mother, from decades ago. When was the last time she'd even seen her face? She couldn't remember.

When Atanas got home that afternoon, she'd asked him.

"Wow, it's gotta be a few years ago now," Atanas decided after some thought. "Roya was still at home, remember? She was on FaceTime with your mom and trying to get her to unmute herself and your mom couldn't figure it out." He laughed. "She didn't know how she'd done it in the first place. After that she said she found FaceTime too confusing and would rather us just call."

Atanas spooned some vegetable soup into a bowl, blowing on it before handing it to Minoo. He'd thrown the ingredients in the crockpot before leaving for work that morning after seeing the cool, gloomy forecast. When Minoo woke, the warm, comforting smell was already blanketing the house. "And you've always said she never really liked being in pictures."

Minoo nodded and sipped at her soup. She tore a slice of crusty baguette in half and chewed absently.

"Don't worry for me," her mother had said before hanging up. "You just enjoy the life you made for yourself."

And the funny thing was, Minoo thought her mother may have actually meant it.

"Hey grandma!" Minoo opens her eyes to find Mrs B looming above us. "Atanas called with the news! Congratulations!"

"Joan, it's your turn!" Minoo lifted her head to see a man in a jaunty fedora poking his head out Mrs B's back door, hollering in their direction. "Joan!" Mrs B waves a hand over her head then turns back to us, fixing her eyes on Minoo. Minoo busies herself arranging my curls.

"Minoo..." Mrs B says.

"JOAN!" The fedora hollers again.

"MARVIN!" She bellows back, startling the hat back into the house. Then softly, "Minoo."

Minoo polishes my eye with her thumb. Its green glares back at her.

Mrs B sighs, then crouches down, her knees cracking. "Oof," she mutters. Her pretty dress billows around her like a bluebell. She clutches the side of the hammock to steady herself and we rock a little. "The things I do for you."

Minoo's dimple twitches. She fusses with my hair. She polishes my other eye. If I had the appendages to knock her hands out of my face, I would.

"Will you at least listen?" It takes me a moment to realize Mrs B is not looking at Minoo. She's looking at me. She places a cool hand on the back of my neck. I pivot slowly. Her thin, silvery eyebrow is raised in an elegant arch. Mrs B, who has never questioned my presence in all these years, but seldom really acknowledged it either, is talking to me.

I manage a nod in response.

"If I've understood correctly, you're here to help Minoo, yes?" I nod again. Realizing my mouth is hanging open, I snap it shut. "I thought so. Cala told me all about you, Ecology Paul, years ago. She didn't want me to get the wrong idea," Mrs B chuckled, "though I'm not sure what the right idea would be. But Cala explained things."

At this, Minoo, who'd been staring through the netting of the hammock, feigning intense interest in the grass, whips her eyes up to Mrs B.

Mrs B waves off her concern and addresses me again. "That's not what I'm trying to talk about. And Cala was only trying to help me understand you. Both of you. And I want you to know I see you. I don't want you to think I haven't. It's just that I've never been sure how much my seeing you does her any good." She tilts her head to Minoo. "You know what I mean?"

She doesn't wait for a response, which is fine because I don't know what to say.

"It's just that I've never wanted to… I've never known…" A breeze rustles the leaves, combs through the fine hair on Minoo's forearms. Mrs B closes her eyes and inhales. "It can be difficult," she whispers. Her eyes, when she opens them, are jewelled blue. "But I think you always try to have her best interest at heart. I think you try to protect her."

I can feel Minoo staring at me, willing me to turn to her, but I keep my gaze tethered to Mrs B.

"All I want to say is, for what it's worth, I think you've done a good job, but I also think Minoo needs to start hearing the truth. The plain truth. No dressing it up. No comparing oranges to organs." Mrs B pushes herself up to stand, wobbling a little before regaining her balance. The squeak of the side door announces the return of the fedora.

"I'm coming, I'm coming!" Mrs B calls. "And you two,"—she spins back to us— "at least one of you has a better place to be. Don't make me come back over here and flip you out of this thing."

We watch her sashay straight-backed to her house.

"You know she will," I say to Minoo.

Minoo sighs, then rolls us out of the hammock, landing on all fours. She stands and brushes the moss and dirt from her knees, then out of my mouth. As we move out from under the groggy shade of the maples, the world feels subdued, in the process of distilling the smudge of midday into something clearer. The sky has deepened from its brittle blue. Minoo checks her watch. It was only two hours ago we left for the hospital.

When Roya last came to visit all those months ago—after she'd slammed out of the house, Charlie in tow—they didn't actually leave right away. She'd looped around back and sat on the stone bench by the herb garden, where, as a child, she spent hours playing in the evenings. The garden had a small, ornamental, solar-powered fairy cottage that would light up when the sun went down. Minoo told her this meant the fairies were home, and if she was very quiet and didn't disturb them, she might even see one. Roya sat on the bench that day with Charlie. Minoo didn't realize where they were, until she heard their voices drift through the open kitchen window.

Minoo looks up at the window now, closed against the afternoon's heat. Lace curtains drawn. The spicy fragrance of lemon balm and chives and rosemary blooms around us. When Roya was here, it was still early spring, and the earth in the gardens was meek brown and produced only scant sprouts here and there, hyacinths yet to break ground, where soon there would be dozens of them. In autumn, for many years when Roya was younger, she and Minoo would plant the bulbs of their spent Nowruz flowers in the gardens. The tulips went in the front flower beds, and the hyacinths—mostly blue, because they were Minoo's favourite—would go in the back gardens, and when they bloomed, they drenched the air in their filmy sweetness.

"I don't know, Roya." Charlie's voice was deep, soothing. "Your mom's quirky, sure, but she's not crazy or anything. They're just puppets. People have hobbies."

Minoo was standing in the hall. She could see many of her creations from there. We were in the family room, the dining room, the living room, and even—if she tilted her head a little to the right—my spot, in the kitchen. An infestation. To be honest, she was a little tickled by this term, creative as it was. A circus. A dawdle. A crash. A pride of puppets. A ragtag collection of hopeful, but slightly tattered, dreams.

Hearing Charlie's voice snapped Minoo out of this reverie. When she heard Roya's reply, she began moving toward the kitchen. The movement was involuntary, because she already knew what she'd heard and knew that what would come next would hurt.

"Easy for you to say," Roya snorted. "It's a charming personality peccadillo until you have to live with it. Remember, I have had to live with it all my life. Can you even imagine?" Atanas was in the process of closing the window when Minoo stepped into the kitchen, but she heard the rest anyway. "Trust me. The woman's nuts."

Minoo remembered the day Roya was born; how hot she'd been when she was placed, wet and wailing, on Minoo's bare chest.

The house was freezing. Minoo shivered.

That night in bed, Minoo reached for Atanas before he fell off the edge of consciousness into sleep. He responded, his body as ready as ever. Rolling onto her, he kissed her eyelids. Her nose. Her neck. He slid her cotton shorts down and ran his hand up the inside of her thigh. How gorgeous it was. How Minoo wanted to weep with the beauty of it—of him, and how she'd wasted it, for so long.

This longing.

The first giggle caught them both by surprise. At first, Atanas must have thought this was a response to his touch—excitement, perhaps. But as he touched her more, she unleashed a flood of laughter. Atanas stopped and reached across the bed to turn on the bedside lamp. In the wash of soft amber light, he considered her thoughtfully. Brushed her hair back from her face.

"My love," he said.

She mashed her fist to her face to try to stop the laughter. This is when he saw me: I'd been there, the whole time. Atanas had put up with a lot over the years, but this was a first for us both.

"I don't wanna be here any more than you do buddy," I said.

Minoo's body heaved, trying to choke down her sobs, tears mixed with laughter now. Atanas lifted himself off of her, gently, then just as gently, he pulled me off her hand and lay me on the bedside table. He propped himself up on the pillows and pulled her to him. The compact warmth of his body. His scent, a lemony musk. The emptiness inside her. He kissed the top of her head and stroked her arm and allowed her to be, as she needed to be, for as long as she needed him.

We've been lingering outside for too long. Minoo shifts from foot to foot. She needs to use the bathroom and has been warned about holding. It could make her down-there problems worse. But inside the house are choices that must be made, and as long as we're outside, we haven't had to make them.

AN ORANGE IS NOT AN ORGAN

The kettle's on. Bladder empty. The bird in the cuckoo clock chirps 5 p.m. Minoo has been thinking about how she needs to call Cala and let her know about the baby. Needs to let her know about everything, and how she doesn't know what to do. Needs her in the way we never stop needing our mothers. The home phone rings.

"Minoo!" Atanas exhales when Minoo answers. "I've been trying to reach you for over an hour. Don't you have your cell on?"

Minoo's mind flies to the upstairs bathroom. She'd taken her phone out of her back pocket when she went to pee but hadn't checked it. It must be on silent, for how long, she couldn't say. This morning Charlie had called the landline to let them know the baby had arrived, and Minoo was the one to call and notify Atanas, who was at the grocery store getting feta cheese for a salad he was making for dinner. Since the store was less than a minute from the hospital already, they'd decided he should just go and Minoo would meet him there.

"The midwife gave us the all-clear and we're on our way to the house. Roya and Charlie are ahead of me. She's agreed to come see you, but I need you to be there, fully. You understand? I love you—we love you—and need you and only you to be there when we get home. We're five minutes away."

Minoo sprints upstairs to the bathroom and finds her cell on the bathroom counter. Four texts, two missed calls. There's also an email notification.

Minoo reads the texts.

> Minoo, Roya loves you and was just upset. I'll talk to her. Charlie's talking to her too. I'll call you in a bit.
>
> Baby has a couple more tests to pass, and we'll be out of here soon.
>
> Minoo, call me when you get home.
>
> Minoo?

The quiet of the house. It settles like dust in our ears. A silence that cuts through this static of feeling. An email… Outside, Minoo hears the shudder of a car engine turning off. The crunch of a second set of tires pulling in the driveway.

She races to Roya's room and looks out the window. Charlie is already out of the car, opening the back door. Roya emerges from the passenger side. Her thick hair is braided into a long rope and over her shoulder. The dress she's wearing is loose and delicately patterned—little blue flowers maybe. Its deep blue brings out the rapt brown of her skin. Minoo remembers this: how her daughter's skin absorbs summer. Its heat and radiance. She can see her daughter, as she was as a child, playing in this front yard, her laughter fresh and clear as sky.

A muffled squawk sounds. From the backseat, Charlie reappears with a small lump held to his chest. It sounds again: that unmistakable newborn bleat. Minoo's heart thrills. Roya rounds the car and takes the bundle—the baby. She cradles the back of its head in one hand, its bottom in the other, and brings her child in front of her so they're forehead to forehead. The baby quiets.

Her child.

Her child and my child.

Roya sways her body, closing her eyes. Minoo closes her eyes. She sees them. Davood and Roya. Her babies. The fathomless pitch of their eyes. The sweetness of that shared air. All those moments and minutes and hours.

"Time has been wasted, but that's not the same as it being too late, Minoo." I say. An orange is not an organ.

Minoo drops me to her side and reopens her eyes. Roya is pecking her child on the nose and tucking the small mound of body into the crook of her arm. While Charlie disappears behind the open trunk, Roya walks over to Willow. She places her hand on the tree. Atanas comes up behind her and says something that makes her smile. A smile as familiar to Minoo as any in its mischievous lopsided perfection.

Minoo can see her take a deep breath before turning to the house, her eyes trailing over the front porch then moving higher. Minoo rolls to the side of the window.

Closer to the house now, their voices. Minoo peeks out and sees Roya and Atanas at the foot of the front steps. Atanas is pointing to the flower beds and Roya is nodding along. And while Roya nods along, the baby, bonneted and rosy, squints up at the window Minoo is peering out of—its mouth a penny-sized O. Even though Minoo knows the child can't see her, not really, she sees the baby. That's what matters. That's what changes everything; this feeling in my fibres. The slow disintegration of being. The clear space between bird call and answer.

The trunk slams. Minoo startles, then looks at me only once, quickly, before shoving her phone in her back pocket and bolting out into the hall. She rips me off her hand, opens the closet door and hurls me into the darkness—in with the others, and the odds and ends she can't decide if she wants anymore. I hit the wall and flop into a dusty nest of detritus, listening to the disappearing rush of footfall down the stairs, across the foyer, toward the front door. Minoo didn't give this much thought. Didn't let me say goodbye. Not even a word. The kettle begins to shriek in the kitchen. The front door clicks open. This is an oversight, all things considered, she may regret later. And this is an oversight, all things considered, that's probably for the best.

ACKNOWLEDGEMENTS

Thank you to Adele Wiseman and her wonderful memoir of motherhood, being a woman, and creativity, *Old Woman at Play*, and thank you to Elizabeth Greene for introducing me to Adele. Thanks also to Lucy E.M. Black, Margo LaPierre, Kevin Wilson, Babak Lakghomi, Gina Leola Woolsey, Khashayar Mohammadi, Lily-Nilofar Soltani, Lindsay Wong, Wayne Ng, Sarah Marie, Allison Snelgrove, Ashley Van Elswyk, Michelle Hardy, Ellie Hastings, and everyone else who read part or all of the manuscript and offered feedback and encouragement.

Thank you the Ontario Arts Council for funding this project. Thank you to Aimee Dunn, my wonderful editor, and to everyone at Palimpsest Press for loving Minoo and Ecology Paul as much as I do. Huge shout out to Selena Mercuri and my colleagues at River Street for the support!

Finally, thank you to my family who put up with me talking to a sock for a year.

Hollay Ghadery is an Iranian-Canadian multi-genre writer living in Ontario on Anishinaabe land. *Fuse*, her memoir of mixed-race identity and mental health, (Guernica Editions 2021) won the 2023 Canadian Bookclub Award for Nonfiction/Memoir. She is the author of *Rebellion Box* (Radiant Press, 2023) and *Widow Fantasies* (Gordon Hill Press, 2024). She is a host on The New Books Network and HOWL on CIUT 89.5 FM, and the Poet Laureate of Scugog Township. Learn more about Hollay at hollayghadery.com. *The Unravelling of Ou*, is her debut novel.